NO ☐ OR RESALE

Mark Hardin,
The Giant Killer

Moving with feline speed and well-conditioned reflexes, N'Cromo followed up his attack with a fast butt stroke to his opponent's head. The tactic would have succeeded if the Penetrator hadn't been even faster and better trained than the Zulu.

Mark bent his knees and ducked beneath the sweeping shotgun stock, then he instantly drove a *seiken* punch between the tall man's legs. The big knuckles of the first and second fingers of Mark's fist struck with piston force, literally bursting N'Cromo's testicles. The giant gasped in utter agony, his seven-foot frame paralyzed by unbelievable pain.

The Penetrator rose between N'Cromo's extended arms, pivoted, and seized the shotgun in a single fluid move. N'Cromo still held the weapon tightly in his fists, his grip increased by the tenseness of his muscles after the karate punch to his groin. Mark suddenly dropped to one knee, pulled the dazed African forward to hurtle over his arched back. N'Cromo's shoulder blades slapped the floor, the impact forcing his breath from his lungs.

BR. 99 POPPY FUND
BELLEVILLE

THE PENETRATOR SERIES:

ATTENTION: SCHOOLS AND CORPORATIONS

PINNACLE Books are available at quantity discounts with bulk purchases for educational, business or special promotional use. For further details, please write to: SPECIAL SALES MANAGER, Pinnacle Books, Inc., 1430 Broadway, New York, NY 10018.

WRITE FOR OUR FREE CATALOG

If there is a Pinnacle Book you want—and you cannot find it locally—it is available from us simply by sending the title and price plus 75¢ to cover mailing and handling costs to:

    Pinnacle Books, Inc.
    Reader Service Department
    1430 Broadway
    New York, NY 10018

Please allow 6 weeks for delivery.

_____Check here if you want to receive our catalog regularly.

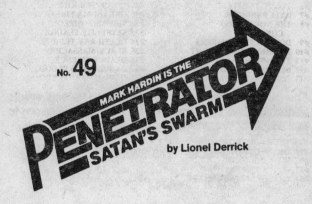

No. 49

MARK HARDIN IS THE

PENETRATOR

SATAN'S SWARM

by Lionel Derrick

PINNACLE BOOKS   NEW YORK

This is a work of fiction. All the characters and events portrayed in this book are fictional, and any resemblance to real people or incidents is purely coincidental.

PENETRATOR #49: SATAN'S SWARM

Copyright © 1982 by Pinnacle Books, Inc.

All rights reserved, including the right to reproduce this book or portions thereof in any form.

An original Pinnacle Books edition, published for the first time anywhere.

Special Acknowledgement to Mark Roberts.

First printing, January 1983

ISBN: 0-523-41681-4

Cover Illustration by George Wilson

Printed in the United States of America

PINNACLE BOOKS, INC.
1430 Broadway
New York, New York 10018

SATAN'S SWARM

NOT FOR RESALE

1

FREE A MONSTER

Even a quiet, natural death would have disturbed the leaden stillness of the stygian, rain-slicked Illinois night.

A large, squarish, white-painted van that resembled a private ambulance ghosted to a squelching stop. Thin lances of water spurted from under the tires and spattered with unusual loudness against the black macadam roadway. The three occupants remained silent, their bodies strained in rigid, forward-leaning postures that projected the latent menace of the potent gods of a lost civilization, carved in volcanic stone by forgotten artisans. Their rasping breathing stilled while they waited.

Down the road, headlights briefly flashed, on—off—on—off, from within a pool of deep shadow under a cluster of aged buckeye trees. The driver put one large, heavy black hand on the shoulder of the man seated next to him. He nodded toward the distant signal.

"They are here." His voice grated loudly in the heavy silence.

"¡Bueno!" The single word came more as an expletive than an observation.

A moment later two men emerged from the nigrescent void under the spreading limbs and walked toward the van. They passed by the cab without a sign of recognition or gesture of greeting to the men inside and entered the rear door of the vehicle.

"Go help them make ready, Raul," N'Cromo, the driver, ordered the slightly built Latino beside him.

"*Sí, teniente,*" Raul responded. He turned sideways and worked his way through the narrow opening into the back of the van. "*Hola, amigos,*" he greeted the arrivals. "*¿Qué tal? Aquí estan los fusiles y las balas.*"

In the front, the driver turned to the remaining man and spoke in the *Farsi* dialect of Arabic. "Are you sure these three are the best men available?"

"Yes, Lieutenant N'Cromo. Their training was personally supervised by the project director, Colonel Po."

"They had better be, Hassid. Our future, and that of the entire operation, depends on how well they perform their duties during the next ten minutes." He started the engine and engaged the gears.

Slowly the van began to wind up a narrow, twisting road toward a wide belt of tall trees that masked from view Hargate State Hospital for the Criminally Insane. The state of Illinois had chosen this obscure, out-of-the way place to hide away its least desirable citizens from embarrassing public view. Beyond this arboreal screen, a tall fence, pierced by forbidding granite pillars and a high iron gate, denied further passage. A sentry box was built into one of the stone buttresses. At the appearance of headlights, a uniformed security man stepped out of the cubicle and squinted to identify the approaching vehicle.

"Got one who went fruitcake in the Westford County Jail," N'Cromo announced in a passably American accent while leaning out the side window. "Supposed to bring him up here for restraint and observation." He waived a sheaf of papers at the guard behind the framework of metal bars.

"That's funny . . ." The sentry's Midwestern twang assaulted the big black man's ears. "Never got no word on that. I'll have to call up to the office, see if the duty doc has anything."

Raul Contreras slipped through the rear door, avoided the step-formed back bumper, and went around one side of the van. Four brisk strides brought him to a place near the cab. Before the security man realized Raul had approached within three feet of him, the Latino raised a silenced .22 pistol and shot the middle-aged man twice between the eyes.

The poison-filled hollow-point bullets did their work almost instantaneously. The guard staggered backward and raised a tentative hand toward the pain in his forehead. He gasped and went rubber legged. His body made a soft, plopping sound when he hit the ground. Raul tucked the fat-snouted handgun into his waistband and ran to the gate.

He easily passed his slightly built form between two upright bars and entered the hospital grounds. He dragged the corpse of the guard to one side and entered the sentry box. There he located the release button and pressed it.

An electric motor whined and the heavy gates swung inward, providing access for the van. Raul remained at the gate while the rest of the team advanced on the low, modernistic cluster of buildings at the hill's crest.

Willamae Johns had been a psychiatric-ward nurse for the past fifteen of her twenty-one years in her chosen career. She liked the work. At forty-four, she still had the stamina and appearance of a woman ten years younger and the strength of a man in his mid-thirties. She could handle the wild ones and mother the befuddled ones. She weighed one hundred sixty-five pounds, deceptively distributed about her large-boned, five-foot-nine frame and, praise be, not a strand of gray yet invaded her glossy, ebon hair, which she combed severely back and swept up under her pert, blue-bordered, white nurse's cap. She had completed her routine round of the sedated patients only a minute before and now moved silently down the hall in her rubber-soled, white oxfords, toward her station at the intersection of A and B wings. A brilliant sweep of headlights across the building front caught her eye through the barred second-floor window.

"Now what?" she queried aloud, resigned to this interruption of accustomed routine. Whatever, it might prove to be interesting. If it meant a new patient, she fervently hoped he wouldn't have to be fitted with a relief tube like that creep Raymond Barr. Mad scientist, indeed!

Doctor Raymond Barr he insisted on being called during his few hours of lucid consciousness each day before the inevitable onset of raving and habitual return to heavy sedation. She could do without that kind on her ward. Willamae securely locked the round iron-barred grille of the Maximum Security Ward cellblock door and headed for her desk. The night bell pealed alarmingly and Willamae heard the strident scrape of wooden chair legs when Pete Chalmers, the inside security man, rose from his desk to go answer the summons.

Pete Chalmers hated his work, hated having to be around nutsy people, and hated most of all the thick-lensed eyeglasses that had forever kept him off a real police force and relegated him to this State Correctional Officer job at a dingbat farm. What the hell, though. How could a guy of fifty-three quit and start over? Who'd hire him?

His bursitis hurt him and his feet had swollen to painful lumps in his tight-fitting shoes through hours of sitting with nothing to do. Could be whoever it was leanin' on the bell out there would bring him something interesting. Maybe another freaky asshole like

Charlie Manson. Those idiots in California. Shoulda locked that Manson up in the screwball ward instead of prison. Better still, blown his ass away. Pete reached the door and yelled out his irritation.

"All right, all right. Get off the fuckin' bell. I'm comin'."

When he climbed from the rear of the van, Juan Rubio shivered in the chill, damp air. Damn this cold, miserable Yankee *gringo* land, he thought. Whoever would want to live here? Not at all like the jungles and mountains of his native country. Juan had been cold since they arrived two days ago, and the open, rolling, treeless plains had made him feel uncomfortable, exposed, and vulnerable. The truly cold weather was supposed to be over, he had been told. March was the start of Spring. Then why did he feel this way? Juan shook off his discontent and eased back the slide on his suppressed Model 59 Smith & Wesson.

A soft metallic whisper accompanied the sliding of a 9mm round into the chamber. Beside Juan, Trinidad Alvedo smiled grimly and drew back the cocking knob on his American 180. The .22 caliber, full-auto weapon spit out slugs at an incredible 1,700 rounds per minute.

If police or soldiers guarded the buildings, they would have no chance against such a firearm. Juan Rubio and Trini Alvedo had grown up in the same village. They had run together, barefoot and naked, through early childhood and survived the worst the jungle could threaten. In their eighth year they had been forced into some semblance of clothing and introduced to the first of four years of schooling. Juan, always short, stocky, and well muscled, had fought all of the schoolyard battles for the inseparable pair. Trinidad, liana-vine thin, with long, spindly arms and legs, had been a budding genius and the natural scholar of the duo.

Had they been born in a larger city, Trini might have gone on to complete his education, perhaps even to the university. As it was, they both became *campesinos* and picked coffee beans and bananas for other men on the big plantations. Then came the revolution and they joined the army of liberation.

There they met Raul Contreras. He filled their minds and fired their spirits with visions of land of their own. The great *fincas* would be wrested from the grasping hands of the oppressive aristocratic landlords and distributed to the people. The corrupt government would be toppled and a true people's council would rule. Raul also spoke of a mighty philosophy, Marxism, which he had learned of while training in Cuba to lead an army of liberation. It promised, Raul assured them, true equality for the people and an ordered society. Personally, Juan thought the description of this supposedly superior social experiment too much resembled the way of life among the many mounds of deadly fire ants that infested the jungles near their home.

Trini, on the other hand, grew more excited with every revelation made by Raul and others regarding the institution of an enlightened Marxist state to rectify the wrongs of the past in their country. He asked questions, avidly read books and pamphlets, and argued endlessly with his fellow peón-soldiers. Had they not succeeded in repulsing the *guardia nacional* and sending the Somozas into exile, Juan firmly believed that Trinidad's excessive zeal would have gotten them both killed. Now, here they were in this strange, alien country, preparing to break a man out of a prison hospital. Of what possible use could this *gringo* doctor be?

Juan dismissed the question with a shrug, nodded to Trini, and they walked around the rear of the van. At the steps that led to tall double doors, they were joined by Boro N'Cromo and Abu Hassid. Together, the four men approached the front entrance to Hargate State Hospital.

* * *

Pete Chalmers twisted the knurled knobs of two dead-bolt locks and swung open the front doors of Hargate State Hospital.

"You picked a hell of a time to bring one of those loonies—" he managed to get out before Juan Rubio raised the bulbous snout of the suppressed 9mm Smith & Wesson and shot Pete in the chest.

Pete staggered backward. The bullet had missed his heart, the powerful slug driving through his left lung and out his back to crack noisily off a thickly plastered wall. Pete cried out in shock and surprise and clawed for the .38 Colt in his belt holster. Juan shot him again.

This time the 9mm pellet smashed into Pete's face, momentarily bulged his eyes from hydrostatic shock, and exploded out the top of his head, carrying away his blue uniform cap. Pete abruptly sat down spraddle-legged on the floor, and a soft grunt forced between his lips in a bubble of blood. Pete's .38 discharged in his dead hand and the unaimed, copper-jacketed slug bit agonizingly into Trini Alvedo's left thigh. Then Pete toppled sideways.

Quickly the four armed men entered the building, Alvedo limping painfully.

"What's going on here?" A white-coated doctor, the night-duty medico, stepped out of his office and shouted his demand at the intruders.

"Take us to Doctor Raymond Barr," N'Cromo demanded. His words had the clipped quality characteristic of the English public school speech.

Dr. Michael Anderson studied the grim-looking gunmen. The one who had spoken, an incredibly tall black man, competently held a short-barreled, police riot shotgun in his hands. He gestured peremptorily with the ugly muzzle and the young psychiatrist cringed. "Are you out of your minds? The man you want is in the maximum security ward, under heavy sedation. You can't get away with coming in here and trying to murder a patient."

"We're not here to kill him, doctor," N'Cromo explained in a patient manner one would use with a slow-witted child. "We came to break him out. We have killed two of your guards, though, and we won't hesitate to do the same to you. Now take us to Doctor Barr."

Dr. Anderson paled, but his trained mind quickly offered a bold scheme to prevent further carnage. "No. You can't possibly get away. The automatic alarm system has been tripped and the police are on their way." A new inspiration encouraged him. Michael Anderson modulated his voice, producing a confident, nearly paternalistic, gently chiding tone he'd found most effective with the more violent cases in his charge.

"Come now. Let's avoid further unpleasantness. Why don't you surrender your arms to me, now, before the police arrive. I'll intercede for you and see that they do you no harm."

N'Cromo remained implacable. "We want Doctor Barr. Are you going to take us to him?"

"Absolutely not. We are at an impasse, gentlemen. I'm simply going to stand here until the police arrive."

The shotgun blast shattered the quiet of the hospital halls. Forty-one pellets of Number 4 buckshot ripped into Dr. Michael Anderson's chest and flung him backward as though propelled by a steam catapult. Before Anderson's body hit the corridor floor, N'Cromo started for the dead psychiatrist's office.

Inside, the seven-foot-tall African located Dr. Raymond Barr's room in A Wing, on the second floor. He motioned to the others to follow, posting the wounded Trinidad Alvedo on the stair landing to cover the entranceway.

Upstairs, the sound of a single shotgun detonation

NOT FOR RESALE

had alerted Willamae Johns to the danger about to envelop her. She sprang from the sturdy government-issued metal chair, rang the alarm bell concealed below the counter, and looked anxiously toward the elevator door. Footsteps pounded on the stair to her left and Willamae snorted in disgust when she discovered how easily she had let habitual practices deceive her. Everyone used the elevator.

Not this time, though. Three men appeared at the top of the stairs. The one in the lead, a huge black man, rushed toward Willamae. He held a wicked-looking shotgun.

"What are you men doing here with guns?" Willamae demanded with icy authority.

"Doctor Barr. Which way?" the black demanded.

"Leave this floor at once," Willamae shot back in imperious tones.

Without warning, the butt of the shotgun swung toward her head and she tried to duck away. The thick wooden stock caught her in front of her left ear and slammed the sturdy nurse back against her desk. She slumped to the floor and lay unconscious in a slowly seeping pool of her blood.

N'Cromo spotted the small plaque that identified A Wing. He leaned over the counter, retrieved a set of keys from the unconscious nurse, with which he opened the cellblock gate and sprinted along the corridor toward the proper room number. Hassid and Juan followed a pace behind. N'Cromo unlocked and threw open the door to Dr. Barr's cell. Inside, he went to the white hospital bed, where a recumbent form lay under sheets, securely strapped to prevent violent movement. N'Cromo produced a small photograph, compared the likeness with the haggard features of the man, and nodded.

"That's him. Unstrap him and bring him along."

Out in the hall a special-duty nurse stepped out of a

room farther along, where an inmate lay dying, and spoke without thinking. "You there. What are you men doing with that patient?"

Juan turned partway to his right and shot the nurse in the throat. Blood flew in a thin spray and the unfortunate woman stumbled into a wall before crumpling in huddled death on the cold vinyl tiles. Juan resumed his share of the burden of Dr. Raymond Barr and all three terrorists made their way to the stairwell.

Three minutes later, the white van sped away into the anonymous darkness, long before a wailing siren approached Hargate State Hospital, in response to the alarm set off by nurse Johns.

2

RECRUIT A MONSTER

Jungles, Colonel Po Hahn Chau thought, a weary sigh escaping from his thin, colorless lips. Po gazed between the slats of the venetian blind to stare down at the dense foliage beyond. Thick-trunked rubber trees with fingerlike leaves resembled huge artificial plants. Giant ferns jutted from the ground and great clusters of vines and moss were everywhere. The colonel had thought he'd seen the last of such miserable, hostile environments when he'd been ordered to leave Southeast Asia in 1970.

Ho Chi Minh had died and Mainland China's involvement in Vietnam soon lost ground to the better organized and experienced Soviets. Ho had been a cunning fox who'd managed to enlist the aid of both the Russians and the People's Republic without allowing his country to be truly dominated by either. Without Ho's political prowess, the tug of war between the two major Communist powers had shifted in favor of the Soviets. Ah, well, Po reflected, although the Russians were no longer true allies of China, at least they were comrades of the cause. His assignment in North Vietnam had not been to his liking anyway.

Then Lieutenant Colonel Po was an officer in the formidable army of the People's Republic of China, attached to the NVA as an advisor. Advisor! Peking had virtually "issued" him to the North Vietnamese, who then put him in command of a prisoner-of-war camp a hundred kilometers from Hanoi. The job itself had not been distasteful to Po. He spoke excellent English and he despised the capitalist West in general, Americans in particular. Interrogating the U.S. servicemen among the inmates had been a distinct pleasure. The more stubborn the soldier, marine, or airman proved to be, the better Po liked it. His methods involved psychological and physical torture and he seldom cared what information he extracted from his victims. However, the POW camp was located in a stinking jungle—hot, uncomfortable, and lacking in creature comforts Po felt he deserved.

Of course, as commandant, he was supreme ruler of the camp and he could travel to Hanoi any time he wished. Hanoi.

It was a backward, provincial village compared to Beijing or Baotau. Worse, the Vietnamese were the most annoying people of Asia. Their language seemed to be a bastard combination of Chinese, French, and whatever grunting tongue their ancestors had spoken before superior cultures had tried to civilize them—an effort Po regarded as utter folly. They were savages, worse even than Koreans, and their muddled politics clearly reflected this. North Vietnam seemed unable to make up its collective mind whether or not to embrace Maoist or Leninist concepts of Communism. Of course, that was a problem Peking appeared to have these days, Po mused with a sad shake of his sleek head.

Yet, Po's duty in Vietnam had earned him a promotion to full colonel and a transfer to the Social Affairs Department—a branch of the Chinese secret service, operated out of the famous Black House. Unlike most countries, China treated its intelligence operatives with respect and honor, granting them many privileges. Despite his new, exalted status, fate played another sarcastic trick on Po.

His new position of authority led him to a station in the Congo as an "advisor" to the Communist "freedom fighters." African jungles were as hot, sticky, and dangerous as their Southeast Asian counterparts.

Indeed, Po's experience in "jungle combat" and coordinating "subjects of the Third World" had been the prime reason Peking assigned him to his newest mission. One which placed Po once again in a steamy tropical forest.

This time, the situation was far different and more to the colonel's taste. Although he had been locked away from civilization in a remote area of formidable terrain, the conditions were far better. He had an office in a modern building of steel and Plexiglas, furnished with the Formica and plastic comforts that Po, who considered himself a man of the future in a changing world, found appealing. Best of all, the place was immaculately clean, air-conditioned, and orderly. Po liked everything to be in its place, regimented and predictable. Further, his mission had to be the greatest, and most challenging of his career.

Success would surely mean a promotion to general and a crippling—if not totally destructive—blow to the enemies of the People's Republic of China. Despite all the nonsensical charades conducted by diplomats,

Po and his superiors had not forgotten who their enemies were. Although his country had its problems with the Soviets, the primary foe of world Communism remained the capitalist West—especially the United States of America. Abruptly, Po turned from the window.

He bent his tall, lean frame over the desk and began to review the stacks of file folders concerning fifteen years of study, research, and experimentation that had led to what could well be the most bold and ingenious SAD operation of all time. Po smiled when he read: PHEROMONAL REACTION #18, DANGER TO COLONY RESPONSE—AFFIRMATIVE SIMULATION IN SUBFAMILY MYRMICINAE.

Po was a soldier, not a scientist, though after years of association with the entomologists of Project Plague Five, such reports no longer baffled him. The colonel still didn't understand the chemical formula charts or exactly how pheromones worked. That didn't matter. One didn't have to know how a bullet or a nuclear missile operated to use one. Plague Five was better than any explosive projectile. It would place Po in command of the most indestructible army in history. An army with limitless numbers, capable of unbelievable devastation.

For more than a decade and a half the project had been in the works. Selecting the right site for the main headquarters had been a major obstacle, but thanks to the success of the Marxist Sandinistan forces in Nicaragua, an ideal location in the Western Hemisphere had been found. In the desolate jungle hills, the final preparations for Plague Five were nearly complete. There remained but one ingredient to guarantee success and, ironically, a demented American scientist promised to be the solution to that problem. Lieutenant Chung, Po's personal aide, entered the office.

A young, enthusiastic junior officer, Chung would have made an excellent member of the Red Guard back in the sixties. His dedication to the cause of world Communism rivaled Po's. The lieutenant needed to cultivate two character traits for which the Chinese are famous: patience and inscrutability. Otherwise, he was a fine officer.

"You requested my presence, comrade colonel?" the aide inquired, standing rigidly at attention. He had the finely chiseled features and delicate, almost effeminate grace of the southern Chinese.

Po glanced at the digital clock on his desk. It was a product of a decadent West, from a corporation in Texas that, no doubt, repressed and mistreated its labor force; yet Po liked the contraption. Po brushed at his thin line of mustache with long, tapered artist's fingers while he switched his gaze to his subordinate.

"Our guest should have had adequate time to recover from the effects of the sedatives, comrade lieutenant," he declared. "I am ready to see him now."

Chung smiled, revealing small, reptilian teeth. "I anticipated your desire, comrade colonel. The prisoner is already being prepared and he shall be here shortly—"

"Lieutenant," Po interrupted sharply. "Do not refer to Doctor Barr as a prisoner. Not even in Chinese. And *never* anticipate an order from a superior officer. When you have earned a position of command, then you can make command decisions. Until then, you will simply follow orders. *Dung bu dung?*"

"*Hau,* comrade colonel," Chung replied, somewhat crestfallen. "I understand."

"Now, go," Po instructed, rummaging through the folders in search of the record concerning Dr. Raymond Barr.

The small, emaciated figure that entered the colonel's office five minutes later hardly resembled a once prosperous American scientist. Raymond Barr's haggard, bewhiskered face with its sunken cheeks and frightened eyes better suited a skid-row wino. Po rose from behind his desk and gestured at a chair.

"Please be seated, doctor," the colonel invited. "And don't look so nervous. No one has harmed you, have they? I assure you no one will."

"Where am I?" Barr asked, his rusty voice suggested he wasn't sure he wanted to know. "What do you want?"

Po displayed a smile that he meant to be reassuring, but it reminded Barr of a hungry crocodile. The colonel's sleek, angular face seemed incapable of warmth. His hair had been clipped almost to the scalp and the cast of his eyes slanted to such a degree it appeared someone had used a razor on his eyelids. Everything about Po seemed sinister, like Richard Loo playing the Japanese commandant of a POW camp in *The Purple Heart*. Barr, a movie buff, frequently cast people in real life in suitable film roles.

"I'm most impressed by your medical achievements, doctor," the colonel stated, ignoring Barr's questions. "You were formerly a biochemist and a toxicologist for a place called the Croydon Chemical Company. They seemed to have regarded you as something of a genius. You were promoted to head of their research department and, I'm sure, you would now be a man of both fame and fortune if that terrible incident hadn't occurred in Indianapolis, about three years ago, was it not?"

Dr. Barr's already pale complexion acquired a chalky texture. He recalled that night all too vividly.

Dr. Barr and his wife had left Rock's T-Bone restaurant and headed for their car in the parking lot. Then three young toughs attacked them. Three brutes that walked upright. Black men who beat Barr senseless and took Louise with them in the car . . .

"Indeed," Po said in a gentle voice. "The memory must be most painful. The criminals murdered your wife and then walked scotfree from a courtroom. So you joined forces with a millionaire named Joseph T. Armbrewster to claim your own form of justice. With Armbrewster's money to finance your research, you developed a substance called Terminus, correct? This compound caused a form of illness that resembled sickle-cell anemia—an incurable genetic blood disease—in victims who inhaled it. Of course, only blacks and mixed bloods could suffer from this ailment."

"They had to pay for what they did to Louise," Barr whispered, almost savagely.

Po shrugged. "You and Armbrewster intended to wipe out the entire black race throughout the United States—or was it the world? No matter. I suspect it was Armbrewster's influence that turned your personal desire for revenge into such an extremist scheme. The man was a fanatic racist who had long sought to create a white-against-black war in your country. Armbrewster, however, was killed before he could stand trial. So your government made you the scape-goat." Po's voice took on a mock tone of outrage. "Such an injustice! You're obviously a brilliant scien-tist; yet they locked you away in a lunatic asylum . . ." he shook his head in dismay.

Dr. Barr blinked with surprise. Could it be that this hard-faced Oriental might actually understand what had happened? Had he finally found someone com-passionate enough to comprehend the extraordinary circumstances involved?

"Please," the doctor began. "Who are you? What do you people want of me?"

"Of course," the Chinese nodded. "It is time I an-swered your questions. I am Colonel Po, but don't let my military title upset you. I'm in charge of an interna-tional research committee concerned with the better-ment of mankind—not warfare. You will notice that my staff consists of various nationalities, for all countries have one common enemy—*insects*."

"Insects?" Barr's gray eyebrows knitted.

"Indeed," Po stated. "Certainly you must be aware that every year swarms of grasshoppers and locusts destroy thousands of acres of crops throughout the world. Malaria, yellow fever, sleeping sickness, even bubonic plague are still responsible for millions of deaths each year in so-called underdeveloped countries. Were you aware that more than half the deaths in Vietnam before the escalation of the war in the nineteen sixties were due to insect bites? Every year, the common honeybee kills more people than poisonous snakes. Here in Latin America, the Chagas' disease, carried by the 'kissing bug,' claims thousands of lives. For centuries, man's war with the insects has been at best a stalemate, but we are going to change that, Doctor Barr."

"How does that concern me?" Barr inquired. "I'm not an entomologist and my field of toxicology has never dealt with insecticides."

"Do you know what pheromones are, doctor?" Po asked, placing the tips of his slender fingers together to form a small tent.

"I'm a biochemist, of course I know about pheromones," Barr replied. "They're natural chemical substances produced by certain animal life—most notably in insects—that stimulate behavioral reactions in members of the same species . . ." the doctor's eyes widened when he realized the importance of his words and his voice trailed off for a second.

"That's how you plan to control the insect problem throughout the world?" The discovery made him breathless.

"There's already been successful work done in the area," Po smiled. "Though we've far surpassed anything that biochemists and entomologists have accomplished in the past. Doctor Barr," he leaned forward and stared meaningfully at his "guest." "We're standing on the threshold of a new world. A world without famine or disease. Perhaps that's an exaggeration, but surely you can see how drastically these and other problems will drop after we've learned to synthetically produce pheromones that can alter the behavorial patterns of entire species of insects."

"Of course, of course," Barr nodded eagerly. "But why was I chosen to assist in this project? Surely there are others more qualified whom you could have enlisted without—well, going to the efforts required to free me from that hospital and transport me here."

"Don't belittle yourself, doctor," the colonel urged. "You've already proven that you can get results rapidly when supplied with enough equipment and data. That you'll have, I assure you. You'll also be working with some of the finest entomologists in the world. Also, your work in genetic chemistry will be a tremendous asset. Certain types of insects tend to favor the skin pigmentation of specific races. The so-called Brazilian killer bee, for example, seems to prefer black victims—especially those with strong traces of alcohol in their blood."

A cold smile turned Barr's face ugly and for a moment his eyes went blank. "Might be a good way to wipe out nigger winos on skid row."

"Doctor!" Po snapped, then he breathed a sad sigh. "I had hoped you'd managed to overcome your personal prejudices. We are striving to accomplish goals that will improve the world for all of mankind. Can you think of a better way to prove that you are totally rehabilitated? You'll be able to return to the United States a free man." When Barr gave him a blank, disbelieving look, Po went on. "No one would dream of sending the winner of next year's Nobel Peace Prize to an asylum, would they?"

"You're right, colonel." Barr rubbed his hands together with delight. "This is a wonderful opportunity in more ways than one. When do I begin?"

"Immediately," Po replied with another crocodile smile pasted on his face.

Although he felt great pleasure in so easily convincing Raymond Barr to willingly assist them in Plague Five, Colonel Po couldn't help being a bit uncomfortable around the man. It wasn't because Barr was a zealot and possibly even a lunatic. Po had encountered many men who fit those descriptions and often used them in the past. However, the records about Dr. Barr told why his mad scheme for Terminus had failed. A mysterious crime fighter known as the Penetrator had been responsible. Indeed, Po knew about this fabled, apparently indestructible one-man army.

The Penetrator had waged war on practically anyone or any organization that threatened the United States of America. More than once, he'd ruined plans by the People's Republic to bring the United States to its knees. SAD had made quite a study of the Penetrator. Particularly after he had wrecked a previous Sino–Third World plot to control the weather and use it as a weapon.

The man's exploits were incredible, but actual information about him remained scarce. The Penetrator had thus far taken on approximately forty-eight missions and succeeded every time. In each instance he had triumphed over staggering odds. Colonel Po mentally brushed the mystery crusader from his mind. No one could stop Project Plague Five.

Not even the Penetrator.

3

TEST OF COURAGE

Mark Hardin stood on the sand in the small *tienta* ring at Penuelas breeding ranch outside Aguascalientes, Mexico, and carefully studied the young *vacilla* over the top border of the yellow-and-magenta *capote* he held in his hands. *She's going to break right*, he thought.

The young heifer calf didn't disappoint him.

Mark, whom the world knew only as the Penetrator, swung the heavy silk-and-canvas cape in a graceful, billowing motion, first across his body from left to right, then around his side, so that the rounded base flared and directed the calf toward him, then around in perfect deception while he executed the flawless *verónica*. The foot-long, needle-pointed young horns had missed his body by less than three inches. He raised his feet and followed the direction of the charge, hoisting the *capote* to sight the animal again. The hackles rose on the small hump of the heifer's *morrillo* and it bolted forward.

Another perfect *verónica*. The pass had been named for Saint Veronica; Christian tradition maintained that she gave Christ her handkerchief to cleanse His face on His way to the Crucifixion. Mark set up the calf, which was being tested for courage, and executed another *verónica*. Then a *media-verónica* and ended the series with a sweeping *rebolera* that sent the year-old critter back to the pinky-finger-sized pick in

20

the hands of Humberto Moro, Jr., a young, aspiring *matador* who sat atop a blindfolded nag. Well protected by thick, quilted padding, the horse was spared the danger of the thrusting, probing horns when Humberto let her ride the pick in until contact was made. Mark watched the *majoral,* the ranch manager, for the sign to make his next *quite,* or taking away of the calf.

Dressed in a *triaje de corta*—the customary ranchero costume of tight-fitting trousers, ruffled white shirt, bolero jacket, red sash, flat-crown, wide-brim Cordovan sombrero,and high heeled three-quarter boots—the Penetrator would not be recognized this day by those who knew him. He seemed right at home in this assemblage of the famous and near famous of the Mexican taurine world.

Albeit considerably tall for the average *matador,* Mark had a presence on the sand that spoke of practice and knowledge. His six-foot-two frame, slim and well muscled, bent in precise motions, blending man and animal in a symphony of color and rhythm. His dark, coppery brown complexion, black hair, brows, and eyes, and hawkbill nose, products of his half-Cheyenne ancestry, could easily place his heritage with those of the hidalgos and Aztecs, as could his thin line of obsidian mustache and fluent, easy use of Mexican-accented Spanish. It would be highly unlikely that the myriad law enforcement officers of a dozen countries, or the press, would identify this man as the solitary, deadly nemesis of crime they all sought for their various reasons.

Yet, the most wanted fugitive in the world gave not a single thought to this anomaly, nor to the fact that among the invited, socialite guests watching his performance sat the district chief of the Servicio Secreto—the Mexican FBI—two chiefs of police, and a state prosecutor, with their wives and children. Mark's attention remained fixed on one thing, the hundred kilos of black hide and flashing horns that bellowed protest to the irritating pain in its shoulders and pawed the ground with sharp hoofs before charging again.

"*¡Olé!*" Scattered voices cheered among the spectators. Mark had received the calf with a flashy *farol,* a pass that began like a *verónica,* only to whip upward at the most dangerous moment, when the horns were poised directly under the *torero's* right armpit, to swirl outward and overhead in a graceful serpentine figure that ended with the *capote* behind the *matador's* back, at waist level.

"*¡Olé!*" the watchers cried over and over while Mark executed a long series of perfectly connected passes. At last, the *vacilla* stood still, head down, muzzle swinging from side to side, eyeing her tormentors. The Penetrator felt a rare exhilaration. He had completely dominated the deadly animal. What matter what those who knew him in the United States might think.

To the uninitiated, it might appear senseless for a grown man to wave a brightly colored cape at a small, female calf. Worse, yet, to thrust a five-eighths-inch diameter, razor-honed pick an inch or so under the heifer's skin. Not so to the *afición,* the followers of *la Fiesta Brava.* It was believed among bull breeders and those into *tauromaquia*—the art and science of bullfighting—that courage in that special line of Iberian bulls was inherited through the maternal line. Feminists take note, the Penetrator thought with amusement. Therefore, female calves were tested at a young age to determine if they became the mothers of brave bulls—or taco meat. Nothing got wasted on a *ganadería,* and that included Penuelas. Even a cowardly calf could be raised for meat. That didn't include this one, the Penetrator acknowledged when he saw the *majoral's* signal to let the calf have another run at the lance.

"Aaaah-ha! Oooh, *vacilla*," the Penetrator chanted while he took a step forward, then began to cross the heifer's front, moving from left to right, to line the animal up with the *picador*. Suddenly he realized she would break left. Quickly he changed his grip and arm position.

A furry black express train plummeted toward Mark Hardin. With supreme confidence, he took a half step left and brought the *capote* around in a spectacular *chiquilina*. Named for the Mexican *matador* who created the pass, this movement, when properly executed—as the Penetrator did—wrapped the *matador's* body in alternating folds of magenta and yellow from head to foot and the horns passed by only a thin, triple layer of cloth away.

Mark's pass delivered the *vacilla* directly onto the pick.

The crowd went wild.

Back bowed, arm raised above his head in rigid salute, the Penetrator acknowledged the accolades with a small turn in place, then walked, grinning broadly, to a *burladero,* the thick, plank target barricade that allowed access in and out of the *tienta* ring and provided protection to the assistants and those who wished to try their luck in the *pachanga*. Mark exchanged his *capote* for the small red *muleta* and a dull practice sword. Following the ritual, he stepped out onto the sand, removed his sombrero, and dedicated the calf to the person of his choice. In this instance, that was Eduardo Solorsano, a retired *matador* and ranking official of Pedro Domeq distilleries, who had invited Mark to the *tienta*.

The Penetrator turned his back on the audience and tossed his hat over his head in the traditional manner. To scattered applause, he stepped out and faced the speedy, tricky young calf.

He began with a series of chopping, punishing

derichasos, short, zigzag passes designed to force the animal to keep its head down and go where the *matador* wanted it to. Then Mark shifted the *muleta* and drew the calf through a *passa por alta,* pivoted and did another, with the cape starting waist high, then abruptly swinging it up out of sight of the charging *vacilla.* She bellowed her frustration and turned sharply on her antagonist. For five minutes the contest continued, bringing the Penetrator many shouts of praise from the spectators.

Then he found the calf lined up the way he wanted: head hung low, sides heaving from exertion, front feet close together and in line. He slipped the *espada* from the reinforced notch in the *muleta,* fitted his fingers into position, the wooden pommel pressed into the palm of his hand, and brought it to chin level, cape drooping low, distracting the calf. Carefully he sighted along the shining steel blade.

Suddenly, memories of Clemente Sandóval, the Baja bandido with the pretentious name of el Barón de Barranca, flashed through his mind. Sandóval had nearly killed him in that house on Guillermo Prieta Norte in La Paz. Wounded and unarmed, Mark had snatched an *espada* off the wall, distracted Sandóval with some improvised cape work, then dispatched him with a passably good *estocada,* right between the shoulder blades. For a moment, the recollection sent a chill over Mark's body. The hand holding his sword trembled slightly.

Then the Penetrator flicked his *muleta,* poised feet flashing into movement as he rushed toward the charging horns. At the last second, as required with these valuable animals, he dropped the blade and plunged his empty hand down on the calf's hump. Bristly hair brushed his knuckles and he pivoted away. The crowd roared their appreciation. He was awarded two symbolic curled paper ears and a tour twice around the ring.

A wild excitement of accomplishment flushed Mark's face and tingled his body. Eduardo Solorsano brought him a plastic cup filled with Presidente brandy and soda.

"¿*Tienes contento?*" the former matador asked.

"Oh, yes, I am most content," the Penetrator replied after washing the dryness from his mouth with the excellent beverage.

"I mean, are you entirely content with your performance?"

Mark required a second's pause before answering. "No. I did everything I wanted to, only I didn't do it perfectly."

Eduardo smiled with warmth and comprehension. "All you need is practice. Next month is the *Feria de San Marcos.* If you plan to come, stay here at the ranch as our guest. You will be able to fight calves every day if you wish."

"I—I'm honored. If it is possible, I'll let you know." The Penetrator didn't know from one day to the next if he would still be alive, let alone what would happen a month in the future.

"Now, come, my friend. There are only two *vacillas* then there's *carnitas,* music, and lots to drink. Enjoy yourself."

NOT FOR RESALE

Late that night, the Penetrator returned to his room in the Hotel Fransia, in downtown Aguascalientes. The city, located on the Alta Plana high desert between Guadalajara on the west and Mexico City far to the east, was famous for its magnificent grape harvest and the large number of bull ranches. In fact, the six most famous *ganaderías* were all within a few hours' drive. It also boasted the most beautiful and extensive Plaza de Charros, where Mexican cowboys performed incredible feats in rodeos unlike anything seen in the United States. Mark felt well fed and droopingly tired. Partway across the ornate lobby of the Fransia, with its glittering crystal chandeliers and huge mural of the Plaza de Armas as it was two hundred years ago, the desk clerk hailed him.

"*Señor* Parker, there is a message for you."

The Penetrator accepted the folded slip of paper and headed to his room. Once inside, he opened it.

"Call at once. Willard."

That meant trouble somewhere in the world, the kind of trouble the Penetrator handled. Professor Willard Haskins, an eccentric, retired geology instructor, had constructed a fabulous underground mansion in the Calico Mountains northwest of Barstow, California, in the Mojave desert. Broken in body and spirit by the vengeful survivors of a black-market ring that he had uncovered in Saigon, the man who would become known as the Penetrator had been sent to the professor by his former football coach. The purpose had been to restore a young, useful man to life. The result had been the birth of a force for good against evil. The brutal murder of Haskins's niece had formed an alliance between Mark, the professor, and David Red Eagle, a Cheyenne medicine chief who had come to the Stronghold to take charge of the embittered veteran's physical recovery.

Together they formed a triumvirate that would serve as judge, jury, and, when need be, executioner of those who thought themselves untouchable, above the laws of ordinary men. For forty-eight missions, they had served well in this capacity. The message from Professor Haskins could only send Mark into the path of danger and possible death.

The Penetrator got an outside line and, with a series of Mexican operators and many clicks and scratches, finally reached his party. The call went through a safe drop in Los Angeles that automatically relayed the call to the old borax mine in the Calico Mountains.

"Is that you, my boy?" the gray-fringed professor inquired when the Spanish-speaking operator turned the line over to him.

"It is. I did all right today, cut two ears."

"That's a barbaric practice," Haskins responded with heavy disapproval.

"No more so than boxing or professional football. And even then, *el toreo* is not a sport. It's . . ." Mark searched for the proper word, something those who follow the bulls have done for centuries. "It's color and ritual and art and high drama. Oh, hell, I can't defend what I feel in sterile intellectual terms. What is happening up there?"

"Outside of being worried out of ten years' life over you playing around those dangerous horns, something rather surprising has happened. Remember the little man you sent to the rubber room?"

"Barr?"

"The same."

The Penetrator remembered Raymond Barr quite vividly. The murderous scientist had devised a scheme to exterminate all blacks in the United States, with ambitions to go on and "cleanse" the world. Barr's obsession had driven him quite insane, the Penetrator recalled, and his own mission had not ended with apprehending the unbalanced chemist. He listened carefully while Professor Haskins explained.

"Barr has escaped from the hospital where he was confined. More accurately, someone has broken him out. There were some deaths involved and as of now there's no clue where Barr might have been taken."

"Could it be a vengeance thing?"

"I doubt it. I have this—ah, feeling. You'd better cut short your vacation and come back."

"I'll take the bus to Guadalajara in the morning. The

midday Continental flight should put me in Los Angeles around three-thirty the next day. No red-eye service from there to the States."

"Very good. David will meet you at LAX."

"I'll need all the files we have on radical black organizations," the Penetrator began when he had freshened up, changed to Hang-Ten walking shorts and moccasins and settled in at the console in the Operations Room of the Stronghold. Prismatic periscopes, designed on the bottom end like small view windows, brought him a vista of the desert outside. Multicolored hills, cactus, and sand provided eye-easing sights from the walls of the underground mansion.

"Bring what we've got on the more extreme groups on the opposite side, too. We can't overlook the possibility that someone wanted Barr out to continue his grisly work."

"Now even you think something like that could be brewing," the professor observed with a shudder. "The last time he nearly succeeded."

"I'm more inclined to think someone wanted him dead. We can't overlook the other possibility, though. Right now we're operating entirely in the dark. I only wish we had more substance."

"There was a witness, a nurse. She's in a coma presently. If you could contact her, it might help."

"All in due time. Right now let's start on the files."

4

UNLEASH A MONSTER

"Good Lord!" Dr. Raymond Barr exclaimed when he stared into the wire-and-steel cage on an aluminum table in the laboratory.

The creature that sluggishly stirred within the cage seemed the product of a nightmare or a horror movie. In fact, it reminded Barr of the monster in *The Tingler*. Almost two feet long, its serpentine body was thick, green, and slimey, with dozens of stout talonlike legs extending on either side. Antenna stalks jutted from its bulb-shaped head.

"You've never seen a giant Bahamian centipede before, doctor?" a stocky, flat-faced Latino, dressed in a white smock, inquired. "This does not surprise me. They are a rare species. *¡Gracias a Dios!*"

"Thank God, indeed," Barr, who understood basic Spanish, agreed. "I had no idea these things could grow to such a size."

"That one is about normal for the Bahamian giant," the Latin remarked. "Some are almost a full meter in length. It's just as nasty as it looks, too. Oh, the centipede is not a very aggressive creature, but even the smallest are poisonous. Most can't hurt you, because their venom is too weak. This *monstruo,* it is more deadly than most snakes. So, don't pet him, *¿comprende?*"

"You needn't worry about that," Barr assured him.

"You seem to know who I am, sir. What is your name, may I ask?"

"Rafael Gomara," the Latin replied, extending a plump hand. "I was formerly with the department of entomology at the University of Mexico." Gomara neglected to mention that he'd also been a member of the 23rd September Communist League and had fled Mexico City to avoid arrest as a terrorist.

"A pleasure to meet you, Doctor Gomara," Barr told him as they shook hands.

"Just call me Rafael," the Mexican shrugged. "Come, I'll introduce you to some of the others you'll be working with—and you'll get to meet some more of our charming tenants." Gomara tilted his head toward the centipede's cage.

Dr. Barr followed Gomara through the lab. He noticed the equipment with appreciation. A Drehen centrifuge, one of the best in the world, sat in one corner near an IBM computer programed for chemical analysis. There were also the usual beakers, test tubes, and Bunsen burners. Barr recognized the various labels on jars of crystallized chemicals. Some were marked by chemical shorthand, such as NACL, H_2SO_4, and Au, others by their common name. Lindane and chlordane were popular ingredients for insecticides, but the doctor was puzzled by the large amounts of powdered protein, Vitamin E, and magnesium oxide on the shelves.

Gomara led Barr to another section of the lab, where two figures in white smocks observed various insects housed in huge glass terrariums, many the size of a small room. The Mexican introduced Barr to the two men.

"Professor Kowdow is our head entomologist," Gomara explained, referring to a stoop-shouldered Korean with skin that resembled wrinkled, yellow parchment and eyeglasses thick as the bottoms of Coke bottles.

"Great pleasure to meet you, Doctor Barr," the Korean bowed politely. He didn't offer to shake hands.

"And this is Doctor Kassem," Gomara continued, introducing Barr to a tall, waspy Arab with a dark complexion, a hawkish nose, and a neatly trimmed beard. Kassem's smile revealed a set of yellow-and-brown stained teeth.

"How do you like our menagerie, doctor?" The Arab inquired, gesturing toward the cages.

"Well," he began hesitantly. "I haven't—" His eyes turned toward one of the larger terrariums and the sentence froze in his throat.

Within the glass container, the largest hornet's nest Barr had ever seen hung from a small tree planted inside the cage. Perhaps a dozen black wasps with yellow stripes on their conical abdomens hovered in the air near the nest. Barr shook his head with disbelief. The insects were enormous, almost the size of hummingbirds.

"We don't need a TV set to watch science fiction," Kassem remarked. "We merely need to look in these terrariums. Those are a species of wasp recently discovered in Zambia. We haven't given them a proper name yet, so we've called them Hymenoptera X, or wasp X for now. They're quite dangerous—extremely aggressive and poisonous. One sting can be fatal," the Arab grinned. "Needless to say, we don't play much softball in here."

Dr. Barr remained stunned by the sight of the monstrous wasps. He didn't look away from their cage until Professor Kowdow placed a long-fingered hand on his arm. "Let us show you a few less exotic insects that you might already be familiar with," the Korean said. "It may help you to understand the importance of what we are trying to accomplish."

Kowdow pointed at another large terrarium. The bottom was covered by sand four feet thick. Large ant mounds extended from the tiny terrain like miniature camel humps. Barr had to strain his eyes to see the small red insects scurrying about within.

"The fire ant," Kowdow announced. "Subfamily Myrmicinae. Native to Brazil, the fire ant appeared in the United States sometime in the nineteen twenties. It has since spread across the American Southwest at an alarming rate. They are a very destructive species that not only devour man's crops but also consume other insects—often types beneficial to humans. Don't let their small size fool you. The fire ant has a venomous stinger. A single worker ant's sting can kill a baby bird. In massive numbers they can be dangerous. Several deaths have been attributed to fire ants. Since they have no natural predators in the United States, those insects threaten to become a greater problem in the future."

The Korean entomologist led Barr to another terrarium. Inside, thousands of orange-and-black bees, only slightly larger than the common honeybee, buzzed and hovered about a set of wooden hives.

"I'm certain you've heard of the Brazilian 'killer bee,' doctor," Kowdow began. "They don't look terribly frightening, do they? Yet, these insects are highly aggressive and they've already claimed thousands of human victims throughout the world."

"Actually, they aren't Brazilian bees at all," Kassem explained. "The strain was originally developed in South Africa when the fierce *Apis adonsonii* bee, native to that country, was crossbred with the docile *Apis mellifica* of Italy. The goal was to create a species that would be aggressive enough to gather more pollen and produce greater honey than the *mellifica,* yet with a 'personality' that would be buffered enough to make the bees safer to handle. It didn't work very well."

"Why would one species of bee have a more temperamental nature than another?" Barr inquired.

"No one really knows the answer," Kassem replied. "But we suspect it's due to environmental conditions that caused certain evolutionary changes in their behavior. The African bees probably had to become fierce in order to survive, since numerous animals and native Africans have raided their hives for thousands of years. In Europe, on the other hand, beekeeping has been practiced for centuries, and this cooperative domestication seems to have made the insects more agreeable."

"Another entomological puzzle is what makes beestings deadly," Gomara added. "The venom consists of alkaline and acidic fluids. Either substance, by itself, seems harmless when injected into laboratory animals. Yet together . . ." the Mexican shook his head.

"I've been stung by bees and never suffered much of an ill effect afterward," Barr stated.

"That's another question that we haven't been able to answer," Kassem admitted. "Beestings don't seem to cause much of an adverse reaction in most people. Oh, a bit of a lump or a rash, but nothing serious. There have been incidents of individuals surviving hundreds of beestings. Yet, for others, a single sting from a common honeybee can be more fatal than a cobra bite. To contribute to this puzzle, people who have been stung in the past without any evidence of an allergic reaction can mysteriously develop such sensitivity."

"It must have something to do with an individual's body chemistry," Barr mused. "Perhaps the change is due to one's diet or age."

"An interesting theory," Kowdow nodded. "And to research the subject will indeed be a worthy biochemical endeavor in the future. However, right now we're concentrating on using pheromones to alter the behavior of insects."

"I understand what pheromones are and how they work," Barr stated. "Yet, why are they so important in regard to insects? As I understand it, pheromones are present in many other life forms. Fish, birds, possibly mammals."

"In fact, they are probably a driving force in *all* animals," Kassem declared. "Including man. Have you ever wondered why a man will suddenly fall in love with a woman, even if she isn't a great beauty and her personality may leave much to be desired? The cause may be more biochemical than emotional, my friend."

"Let's avoid such theories and discuss insects for now," Kowdow urged. "To answer your question, Doctor Barr, one must understand the anatomy and chemical structure of insects. They are extremely primitive life forms with a very simple nervous system. The brain is little more than a cluster of nerves. In fact, most of the motor responses of an insect are caused by ganglia located throughout its body. With such a simple anatomy, these creatures are incapable of thought. They simply react to instincts that have been programed into them by nature, like miniature computers or robots.

"Now," Kowdow continued as he walked to a cabinet that contained numerous jars of a clear substance that resembled water. "Pheromones are biochemical forms producing a response from a creature based on its evolutionary 'programing.' Since insects can't think, learn, or make decisions, they are unable to deny a pheromonal command."

"Perhaps a demonstration might help to explain pheromones," Kassem suggested, scanning over the jars like a consumer in a supermarket. "Let's see— what about Pheromonal Response Eighteen in subfamily Dorylinae?"

"Threat to colony," Kowdow nodded. "That's always a dramatic stimulus and the *siafu* never fail to perform rapidly."

"Siafu?" Barr inquired, watching Kassem draw a small portion of liquid from a jar into an eyedropper.

"Yes," the Arab replied. "The African driver ant—not to be mistaken with the South American army ant. The latter simply start biting as soon as they find something worth chewing on. The *siafu* are better organized—as you'll see."

Kassem carried the eyedropper across the room to a row of small wire cages. Opening one, he reached inside and, grabbing it by its tail, pulled out a large white rat with small pink eyes. Squeezing the dropper, Kassem squirted the contents on the rodent and carried it to one of the largest terrariums. Climbing on a stepladder, he lifted the rat to the top of the cage and opened a small trapdoor at the roof. Then he dropped the animal inside and closed the lid.

Barr stepped closer and stared into the terrarium, expecting to see its interior covered with giant ants. It seemed to be disappointingly empty, except for some rocks and part of a log placed on a dirt surface. The rat crawled about, examining its surroundings without fear. Apparently, the rodent was glad to get an opportunity for some exercise in such a large container.

"The *siafu* generally reside under rocks and trees by day and only come out periodically in mass numbers—usually at night—to search for food," Kassem explained. "Just watch."

Seconds later the driver ants emerged from their shelter. Barr was astonished by the number of inch-long, dark brown insects that suddenly appeared. Their antennae twitched violently and small mandibles opened and closed while hundreds of *siafu* scrambled toward the unsuspecting rat.

"Bear in mind," Kowdow said, "driver ants are totally blind. They know their surroundings solely by their antennae and they respond entirely to pheromonal commands. See how quickly they've discovered the rat, which they regard as an invader that has attacked the colony?"

Fascinated, Barr watched the ants march to the white, furry creature and rapidly mount its body. The rat didn't seem to notice the *siafu* until they had virtually covered it from nose to tail. The rodent gave a small squeal of fear a moment before the ants began to bite.

"Isn't that extraordinary?" Kassem remarked, calmly watching the rat's thrashing body as the ants continued to swarm over it, tearing the rodent to pieces. "Did you notice how the *siafu* waited until enough of their comrades were in position to attack before they began to bite *in unison?* See how they attack the nose, mouth, and eyes to blind and suffocate their prey? Really incredible, eh, Doctor Barr?"

Raymond Barr did not reply. He had hastily located a waste basket and threw up, covering his eyes with his hands and wishing the rat's squeals couldn't penetrate the glass terrarium. Then the rodent's death cries ceased. Realizing why, Barr opened his mouth and vomited again.

Colonel Po ran the tip of an aluminum pointer along the map of the United States to indicate red triangles pasted on the chart. "These are the bases already established for our operation, comrades," he explained in a voice that revealed pride and a sense of accomplishment. "Insect-breeding centers have been constructed in the southwestern states, as well as in Mexico. In the northern part of the country and Canada, we've concentrated on additional production of pheromones. The reason for this is simply because insects tend to hibernate in colder climates."

The men seated around the long walnut table in the conference room nodded their approval. They were an assortment of Arabs, Africans, Orientals, and Latinos—representatives of seven nationalities. Four of them had been sent by their countries' governments to take part in the scheme. The other three were high-ranking members of terrorist organizations. All were devoted to the concept of international Communism with the Third World collectively ruling together.

Yassine Fawhi, a major in the Libyan army, personally considered Plague Five to be absurd. Only a lunatic like Muammar Qaddafi would have agreed to be part of such madness! Fawhi wondered what sort of maniac conceived the idea in the first place.

"Comrade colonel," the Libyan began. "I regret that I must point out a flaw in this plan. As you say, the colder climates will reduce the activity of these killer insects, so the operation can only succeed in the southern portions of the United States and Mexico."

"During the summer months," Po replied simply, "the Western Hemisphere will be warm enough to assure that *all* species of insects will be active. Have no fear of that, Comrade major."

Robert M'Nobi, a representative from Mozambique, who was terrified the Russians would discover his government's secret agreement with Red China and the other Third World nations involved in the conspiracy, nervously gulped his tea and spoke. "What has me confused, Colonel Po, is how you intend to transport these insects." His voice came in the clipped, British English accent he had acquired when he attended school in Rhodesia before embracing the new "religion" of Marxism when he returned to his native country.

"You can't be sending *siafu* in the bloody mails, you know. What about those monster wasps these mad scientists came up with? Let's be logical about this business, what?"

"The tropical insects will remain in zones that best suit their metabolisms," Po explained. "Besides, few of the insects in our plan will have to be moved anywhere. The pheromones will infect the creatures that already inhabit the countries we intend to attack. True, we can't send driver ants into Ottawa or killer wasps to Seattle, but mosquitoes, lice, fleas, and ticks are already waiting for us to contaminate them with the strains of malaria, typhus, bubonic plague, and other diseases that our people have been working on. With the assistance of the pheromones to direct the insects into densely populated areas, the effect will be the most widespread and devastating bacteriological assault in history."

The colonel slid his telescoping pointer shut and turned to face his fellow conspirators. "Think of it, comrades! Incredible epidemics ravaging the Northwest, swarms of locusts and grasshoppers devouring crops in the Midwest, thousands killed by murderous ants and wasps in the southern states. Famine, death, disruption of communications, financial ruin, and utter chaos throughout the Western Hemisphere. The sheer terror alone will be enough to bring our enemies to their knees. It will be impossible for them to fight our insect minions.

"How can one battle an opponent that numbers in the hundreds of billions? An enemy that's often too small to see until it's literally under one's nose. An adversary that is found *everywhere* and can infiltrate *anywhere!* There isn't enough insecticide in the world to combat them. And, bear in mind, the creatures bred here have been fed small doses of poisons to create immunities as well. They've grown larger, stronger, thanks to special vitamins and crossbreeding of similar species. What will the Americans do? Try to burn

NOT FOR RESALE

the insects out?" Po shrugged. "To do that they'll have to burn their own homes, businesses, and cities to the ground, and even then they won't be rid of Plague Five!"

Po smiled. "It is ironic, is it not? The project that shall destroy America, a country that boasts that it is a 'Christian nation,' has been named for the fifth plague that God and Moses supposedly brought upon the Pharaoh's people in the Bible. The Plague of Locusts. I tell you, comrades, within less than a year the entire Western Hemisphere will be ready not only to surrender to us but to welcome our arrival to save them from their plight."

"Sí, sí," Juan Montoya, a colonel in the new Sandinistan army nodded. "So we get to take over los Estados Unidos—so we, too, can be killed by soldier ants, bubonic plague, and have crab lice chewing our *cojones.*"

Colonel Po shook his head in dismay. Such idiots he had to deal with as allies. Fortunately, the People's Republic would be able to put these barbarians in their place when the time came.

"Comrade Montoya," Po began, refusing to address the Sandinistan by the same rank as his own. "The same pheromonal technology that created Plague Five will also allow us to control the insects after we conquer the Americas. Also, our people will receive the necessary vaccinations to protect us from the various diseases until our entomologists arrange to have all the fleas, ticks, and lice willingly march into the jaws of awaiting spiders and mantises. Plague Five is absolutely foolproof."

Po folded his arms akimbo on his chest and gazed at the others with smug satisfaction. "My comrades," he declared. "We are about to claim the greatest conquest in the history of mankind—without firing a shot!"

5

FALSE TRAIL

"Has the Knighthawk placed all his Kleagles?"

A tall man in a scarlet robe came forward. When he spoke, his high, conical hood, its long wings thrown back from his face, swayed with the movement of his jaws. "Yes, Imperial Wizard."

"And everyone here is under the seal?"

"Yes, Imperial Wizard."

"Fine, then we can begin."

Of the fifty-six men in this large meeting room in a motel on the outskirts of Chicago, only one had his features obscured by a mask. The Penetrator had learned of this high-level meeting of the Ku Klux Klan and, through a longtime friend with connections inside the organization, he had obtained a "passport" to the Invisible Kingdom of the KKK. With it, he had also procured an invitation to this important Konclave and an endorsement, supposedly from the Grand Dragon of California, indicating that the bearer was of such public notice that he must remain, unchallenged, behind a mask. Mark's dark, Cheyenne features would definitely not make him welcome among the gathered Klansmen. The Imperial Wizard, national leader of the Klan, spoke again.

"You all know that the reason for this Konclave is to determine what we can do about an extremely difficult situation." The youthful-looking leader's well-modulated tones and educated speech came as a surprise to the

Penetrator, who more or less expected a group of "y'allin' good ol' boy" type red-necks. "I refer, of course, to the escape of Doctor Raymond Barr."

A Klansman rose near the back of the meeting room. "Before you go any further, Imperial Wizard, I suggest that we ask the Brother from California to remove his face mask. We're all safe here, at least those of us who can see each other are."

"Our Knighthawk has assured me that the Brother to whom you refer is fully authorized to maintain anonymity. For the same reason, he is using an assumed name."

"Now, just what would that be? That reason I mean."

"It has been determined that his public image could be seriously harmed were his connection to our Brotherhood to be discovered by the press lurking outside."

"Ya don't mean that's Governor Moonbeam under the mask?" a comedian near the speaker's rostrum inquired, breaking the growing tension.

When the chuckles died, the Imperial Wizard continued. "Hardly. Anyway, it is a small courtesy. Now to Raymond Barr."

"Any idea who got him out, Imperial Wizard?"

"None. The thing is that sooner or later the authorities are going to come up with the idea we did it. You know that Barr had invented some secret formula that allowed him to kill off niggers without harming anyone else. That's just the sort of insane thing the liberals and the Feds like to try to hang on us. We can't afford to let that happen."

The Penetrator's eyes widened in surprise. His research led him to believe that the Klan, or some other extremist organization, had been behind Barr's escape. And, he had to admit, for the same reasons given by the leader of the Klan. Another Klansman rose.

"What're we going to do about it?"

"We have to find Barr," came the reply. "Not to put

him to work for us but to capture him and turn him over to the law."

"Why would we want to do that?" protested a graying man near the center of the group. "Even if he's crazy, we sure can't object to what he had in mind to do."

"Quite to the contrary," the Imperial Wizard returned. "His kind—and I'm sure most of you will agree—give the Klan a much worse name than it already has. We can't afford the bad publicity.

"I still say I want to see this Californian. How do we know he ain't from the FBI?"

"What if he is? There's nothing illegal about our holding this meeting. And there's certainly nothing wrong with what we propose to do. If anything, it might give us a little better break with the press. If one man wants to remain anonymous, that's his right."

"No it ain't. I don't like the idea of spies. And I never have trusted those Californians. The place is full of fruits and nuts. I'm not sure he ain't here to kill us all."

"Relax, Brother Fulton. We have nothing to fear from this man. We'll say nothing more on the subject. Now, to my proposal. Will the Brothers from Illinois head a search for Barr?"

Seven men nodded in affirmation. "We want him back behind bars bad as you do," their spokesman announced. "If he can do something like that to niggers, who knows what a nut like that will come up with next? Maybe he wants to get even with all whites for putting him in the bughouse."

"Well put. Now, here's how we will handle this . . ."

When the meeting broke up, the press was admitted. The Imperial Wizard read a prepared statement offering the Klan's assistance to authorities in tracking down Raymond Barr. Standing near a camera crew, the Penetrator noticed a short, pert-looking young woman with light brown hair and bright, intelligently gleaming hazel eyes. When she had a chance to insert a pointed, meaningful question relating to the statement, she listened to the answer with total absorption. Occasionally she spoke into the mike she held in her left hand. When the press switched to loaded, biased inquiries, aimed at the Klan in general, the Penetrator took that opportunity to slip out of the room unnoticed.

In a rest room he disposed of his white robe, with its wheeled-circle, cross-and-blood-drop Klan emblem and the other accoutrements of a Klansman. He stepped out into the corridor and was confronted by the young female reporter, an eager, inquisitive expression on her face.

"Hello," she began in a soft, mellow voice that the Penetrator found to be pleasing. "You were at that Klan meeting, right? The—what do they call it?—Konclave."

"What gave you that idea?" Mark Hardin asked in a bland, noncommittal voice.

"Look, I saw this one guy at the press conference. Of all the others, he was the only one who wore a mask. I got curious, so I followed him here. He was big, like you. He went in the john there, no one else has entered, and you're the only one who has come out. One and one still make two, don't they?"

"You've made a mistake."

"No I haven't. I'm Penny Gleason. Maybe you've seen me on WCXT-TV? I'm an anchor person."

"Don't ask me about television. For all I know, an anchor person might be the guy who drops that big hook off a boat. And I don't live in Chicago."

"Aha! Then you admit to being here from out of state for the Klan thing."

"You said that, not I. The man you want is still in there."

"I don't believe that." Penny's face changed, took on a confidential expression, and her voice wheedled. "Hey, you can level with me. I didn't think you belonged with the rest of the white-sheeters. You're not the type. Now that I've had a look at you, it's obvious you're not and why you wore a mask. You're either Sioux or Cheyenne, hardly the basic bedsheet material. What is it? FBI? CIA? Some Senate committee?"

"I'm sorry, but I really have nothing to say."

"You want me to go back in there and blow the whistle on you?" When the Penetrator made no reply, Penny went on. "This Raymond Barr thing is big, right? I can't think of anything else that would get the night-rider set out in broad daylight like this. You were in that meeting, and I know it. Yet you ditched your sheet and hood in the men's room. So you must be some sort of Fed. That makes the story even bigger.

"A break like this could put me in the way of a network job. I mean, this is a tremendous story. If you help me, I'll help you, all right?"

"How, ah, Penny?"

The aggressive reporter smiled. She had him hooked. "Get you some breaks, without destroying your cover. Like I said, I could tip off the Klan boys and really ruin your day. Or—I could give you a bit of information I bet you don't have yet."

Mark smiled. "You keep dangling that bait in front of my face. Spell it out."

"Okay. For starters, I won't tell on you to the Klan. I just got word on my Handie-Talkie that Willamae Johns is now conscious. That's the nurse from the hospital where Doctor Barr escaped. With your credentials, whatever they are, you can get in to see her sooner and easier than the press. Take me along and I keep closed about you."

The Penetrator gave it a long moment's thought.

"I'm Steve Benson, and I think you have a deal, Penny."

The Arness Clinic was located on Lake Shore Drive, probably the most scenic and pleasant section of Chicago. Penny explained that she had friends among Chicago's Finest who kept her informed on breaking stories. Through them she had discovered that Willamae Johns, the nurse who'd survived the raid on Hargate State Hospital, was recuperating at the Arness Clinic. Mark had to admire the young reporter's investigative savvy. Even Professor Haskins hadn't come up with this location.

When they arrived at the small private hospital, Mark showed his identification to the cops on duty. The chubby, moon-faced sergeant with graying hair winked broadly and nodded toward Penny.

"And I suppose Ms. Gleason here is one of your agents. It's okay with me, though. You can both go on up."

A doctor met them on the twenty-third floor and explained that his patient, Ms. Johns, had suffered a severe concussion and a ruptured eardrum. "She took a pretty nasty blow on the head," he offered. "Ms. Johns said she tried to duck the attacker's swing, which probably accounts for her survival. If the blow had been more solidly struck, it would have shattered the temporal bone and possibly cracked the coronal suture like an eggshell."

"I understood she'd regained consciousness, doctor," the Penetrator stated, worried that the boys in blue had given too optimistic an account of the nurse's condition to Penny.

"She has," the medico confirmed. "In a couple of weeks she should be fit as the proverbial fiddle. That's one tough lady. Still, I must ask that you keep your questions brief. She needs rest."

"We understand, doctor," Mark assured him. "If this wasn't important, we wouldn't disturb her now."

"Of course," the medical man smiled thinly. "What could be more important than adding to the grisly details of another crime for the six o'clock news?" he held his eyes on Penny. *Damn!* the Penetrator thought. Did everyone in Chicago know Penny Gleason? "Just make it brief—say, fifteen minutes. I'll be back then."

Penny watched the doctor walk down the corridor. "The nerve of that guy," she muttered.

"Can't blame him," the Penetrator remarked. "He probably sees you as having traduced a federal agent for the sake of sensationalist journalism. Regardless, we can't explain our reasons to him."

"To *him!*" the girl's hazel eyes glared at Mark. "You haven't really told *me* what you're up to yet," her even, white teeth produced a too-sweet smile. "But I'll figure it out."

With that, she and the Penetrator entered Willamae Johns's room. Although the Hargate nurse appeared pale and a bit haggard, Mark noticed the fiery, alert quality of Willamae's eyes. He decided the doctor was right. In two weeks the nurse would be ready to wrestle alligators—and Mark wouldn't bet the reptiles would have a chance.

Willamae wearily recalled the night that Dr. Barr had been abducted from the sanitarium. "I feel rather foolish about the way I reacted when I saw the intruders," she admitted. "Three men armed with guns appeared from the stairwell and I told them to leave as though they were visitors who'd hung around after hours were up. I had been in a small room behind the nurse's station, centrifuging some drugs, so I didn't hear the shot that killed poor Doctor Anderson and I didn't know what I was up against until one of them demanded to know where Doctor Barr was kept. When I refused to answer, he stepped forward and smacked me in the head with the stock of his shotgun. It looked like my husband's twelve-gauge pump, but the barrel was shorter. More like the sort of gun the police use."

"A riot gun," Mark said, pleased by the nurse's keen observations and ability for clear recall. "What can you tell us about the men you saw? Their appearance, speech, whatever."

"Only the man with the shotgun spoke," she replied. "Oh, I'm not apt to forget that one! He was a black man—you'll think I'm exaggerating—but he had to be close to seven feet tall."

The Penetrator's eyebrows rose. "A black man? Are you certain?"

"Of course I am," Willamae insisted, considering Mark's question silly. "Oddly enough, he spoke with a British accent. Almost cultured. I didn't get a good look at the other two men, though I noticed they both carried pistols with silencers attached—like you see on TV. They appeared to be Mexicans or some kind of Latin Americans."

"A black man and two Latinos?" Penny shook her head. "I can't see why they'd break a guy like Raymond Barr out of the bughouse. Barr was sort of a super Archie Bunker, playing with a murderous chemistry set."

"I'm quite familiar with his case history, young lady," Willamae declared testily. "But I'm certain of what I saw."

"Nobody doubts your word, ma'am," Mark assured her. "Is there anything else you can recall?" When Willamae shook her head, he went on. "Then we'd better go and let you rest up. Take care when you get those gators in a headlock. They bite."

The nurse blinked with confusion at the Penetrator's remark, but Mark didn't wait to explain it. He headed for the door, his mind trying to evaluate the startling new information about Dr. Barr's escape, in an attempt to come up with an answer that made sense.

"Where do you think you're going, Steve?" Penny demanded, galloping toward the Penetrator as he marched briskly along the corridor.

"Look," Mark began, wishing the girl wasn't in such good shape. Damn, she could be a champion marathon runner. "I appreciate you not squealing on me, and now you have an exclusive for your story. So I think it's time for us to part company . . ."

"Oh, no you don't!" Penny insisted. "I've got one of those fabulous 'noses for news' they talk about and, unless my sniffer has gone haywire, I've picked up a strong scent for one helluva story—and I think *you* might be part of it."

The Penetrator frowned. With Penny's connections with the Chicago police, he couldn't risk having a scene with the girl. He'd have to let her tag along for a while, until he could lose her later.

"Awh, hell," Mark muttered. "Come on, Little Miss Bloodhound. I'll buy you dinner, if you promise not to gulp your Gravy Train."

Penny crinkled her nose at him with annoyance, but she didn't leave his side.

6

ARACHNID ARMY

Flies darted about like ricocheting bullets equipped with wings. They buzzed fiercely within the small cage while Dr. Raymond Barr connected the container to an aquarium-sized compartment containing yet more insects. Rafael Gomara watched in admiration when the first group of flies swiftly swooped down to specific creatures of their same species, ignoring others in the container.

"The females are mating with the males sterilized by radiation," Gomara announced, peering into the tank.

"How can you tell the difference?" Colonel Po inquired.

"Females don't mate with females and males don't—"

"Spare me your lesson in basic biology," the colonel coldly snapped. "And your feeble attempts at humor, Doctor Gomara. How can you tell which males have been sterilized?"

"The radiation chamber was coated by a white aluminum powder," Barr supplied the answer. "The sterile males have traces on the hairs of their legs. The pheromone I developed attracts females to these males. Note how the insect ladies ignore the other gentlemen flies available for mating. Also, if you'll look carefully, you'll see that a number of different species of the Diptera family are affected by this single pheromone. There are bluebottle flies, horseflies, fruit flies, and even—what's the name of that African fly that causes sleeping sickness, Rafael?"

"Doctor Barr," Po began in a weary voice. "I'm quite impressed by this accomplishment, but I'm certain you're aware that sterilizing fruit flies didn't work very well in California."

"Part of the reason for that might have been a failure in the sterilization process," Professor Kowdow remarked, lighting a long-stemmed pipe. "However, Doctor Barr has done some remarkable work with pheromones the last few days. He is a most gifted chemist."

"No one is doubting his ability," Po assured the Korean entomologist. "And his success here is quite extraordinary, but I'd instructed him to work on the pheromonal responses that make certain insects favor various skin pigmentations, as well as on the feeding, attack, and swarming pheromones the rest of you have been busy with."

"Colonel Po," Barr began, a trace of suspicion in his voice. "I don't understand why you're so concerned with those responses. Surely this," he gestured at the flies in the cage, "is the best way to reduce the insect problem throughout the world—by reducing their population in the future."

Po mentally groped for a reply. Dr. Kassem supplied one before the colonel could speak. "Radiation treatments don't work well with many species of insects, Doctor Barr," the Arab explained. "Despite the nonsense one sees in science fiction movies, insects and reptiles are actually the least affected of all animal life-forms when it comes to radiation. Cockroaches, for example, can absorb enough radiation to kill a score of men; yet they don't seem to suffer in any way. Besides, you can't sterilize enough insects to make any real difference in their population. California is evidence of that."

"The swarming instinct will help us centralize large groups of insects," Po stated, finally ready to verbally defend his position. "Then they can be poisoned or captured for either research or sterilization."

"But why increase their feeding pheromones or the impulse to attack?" Barr inquired.

"By controlling the feeding responses, we can eventually alter the selection of insects' diets," Kowdow claimed. "Think of it this way—a swarm of locusts swoop down on a wheat field, but instead of devouring the grain, they eat only the thistles and weeds. In fact, harmful insects could be turned into friends of mankind."

"As for the attack response," Po began suavely,

"as you know, many insects are natural predators of pests. The praying mantis, dragonflies, spiders—"

"Spiders are arachnids, not insects," Gomara interrupted.

Po glared at the Mexican. "The pheromonal response still applies to them, doctor. That's the point I'm trying to make to Doctor Barr. Making these creatures more aggressive will reduce the numbers of their harmful relatives."

"I see," Raymond Barr sighed. "Very well, colonel. I'll concentrate my efforts in the areas you desire." He smiled weakly. "You gentlemen are paying the bills, right?"

Colonel Po sat behind his desk, mechanically cleaning a disassembled Spanish Astra .380 automatic. The "Constable" was a better weapon in every way than the Chinese version of a Russian Tokarev Po had been issued as a sidearm, which had remained locked in a desk drawer since he'd gotten his hands on the Astra. When they seized the United States, Po thought, he'd have a vast selection of excellent weapons to choose from. Americans manufactured so many fine firearms of such a wide variety. Most of these guns were in the hands of the civilian population—a fact that made invading the United States by conventional means impossible. How can one conquer a nation of 280 million where virtually everyone has the capability of shooting back?

That was one of the main reasons Peking conceived Plague Five. Bullets, tanks, missiles—all would be useless against swarms of killer insects. Of course, the Chinese occupation forces and their Third World allies would still have to deal with any resistance movement that might arise in the United States after the country had been seized. All those privately owned firearms meant the conquerors would have quite a problem to deal with. However, that would be some-body else's problem. Po would return to China—to receive a promotion and a new position, hopefully at the Black House in Peking, where he'd finally been able to spend some time with his wife and three children, whom he hadn't seen in five years.

First, Plague Five had to succeed, he realized, and part of that success depended on Raymond Barr. Although a lunatic, the biochemist's ability in research and development of new chemical compounds was extraordinary. Barr's new fly-mating pheromone was proof of that.

Yet, this wouldn't help their plans for invasion. Colonel Po cursed under his breath and began to reas-semble the Astra pistol. All the preparations for Plague Five were in the works. Direct action could begin immediately. Everything would run like a well-oiled machine if Barr provided them with the final, essential cog they needed.

If he failed, Plague Five might drag on for months before Po's people could enlist another chemist with Barr's qualifications to solve the problem. How long would it be before the insect-breeding compounds or chemical production centers scattered throughout the Western Hemisphere were discovered? Po's expres-sion hardened. They didn't have months to spare. Plague Five had to begin soon or—

The office door opened and Lieutenant Chung quickly entered. Po looked up with surprise. His aide had ignored proper procedure and common manners to enter unannounced, though Po wasn't angry. Chung must have a reason for his conduct and the pleased expression on the lieutenant's round face suggested he might be the bearer of good news.

"Comrade colonel," Chung smiled. "I am most happy to report that Doctor Barr's efforts to produce the synthetic chemical for Pheromonal Response Twenty-Seven has been successful!"

Po's head snapped back as though the news served as a verbal slap in the face. It in fact had. "Are you certain, comrade lieutenant?"

Chung nodded. "Tests are conducted with various insects on skin samples of different races. The American *has* found the key to attracting the creatures toward specific pigmentations and how to prevent them from attacking other skin types."

"How many species of insects can be controlled by this chemical?" the colonel eagerly inquired.

"Twelve have been successfully tested, comrade colonel," Chung declared. "I'm not certain of their names, but they're ants, bees, and wasps. Barr said certain variations will be needed in the compound, but he feels positive others can likewise be controlled."

"*Han hau!*" Po exclaimed with approval, slipping the Astra into a button-flap holster on his hip. "We must contact the other posts and begin Project Plague Five the moment we can transport the pheromones to them."

"What about Barr?" Chung inquired. "It seems to me we no longer need the American."

"No," the colonel insisted. "The doctor's work isn't completed, and he's too valuable to execute at this time."

"But, Comrade Colonel, he seems suspicious of our true motives."

"He isn't that suspicious or he wouldn't have cooperated this far," Po shrugged. "According to Barr's file, he has a weakness for alcohol and he apparently developed a taste for marijuana and young girls when he was in Puerto Rico working on the Terminus compound. Barr seems to get along well with Gomara. I'll tell the Mexican to supply our American friend with some of his favorite intoxicants to celebrate his new breakthrough. And send to the village for some little girls, say eight to eleven years old. We'll keep Barr pacified just enough to control him. Besides, the man might be a genius in the laboratory, but he lacks the qualities of cunning and courage required to be truly dangerous. We can afford to keep him alive for a while."

"Of course, comrade colonel," Chung agreed. He frowned slightly. "We also received a radio message from that African in the state of Illinois. The one that commanded the abduction of Doctor Barr."

"Lieutenant N'Cromo," Po nodded. "He's a most competent man, considering he's part of such an inferior race. To think those apes actually believe we'd let them rule with us as equals! Still, they've been useful from time to time and N'Cromo is an exception compared to most of his kind. What does he have to report?"

"It seems the police aren't the only people interested in the disappearance of Doctor Barr," Chung replied. "N'Cromo claims a pair of investigative reporters managed to interview a woman witness who survived the raid at the insane asylum."

"A survivor?" Po frowned. "I thought the lieutenant had killed anyone who might have identified Barr's abductors."

"N'Cromo believed he'd killed the woman with a butt stroke to the skull," the aide shrugged. "She was in a coma for several days but recovered recently. I knew we shouldn't have trusted a *hai dung-wu* with a position of responsibility. Africans are incapable of handling command."

"Lieutenant N'Cromo speaks three languages fluently and he's proven himself to be an effective and resourceful guerrilla fighter both in the jungles and the cities," Po interrupted. "Don't disregard the man because he made one mistake. Why does N'Cromo think a pair of investigative reporters are a threat to us? Surely, the police will learn the same information from this witness."

"The Chicago police seem to feel Doctor Barr was taken from the asylum by some sort of militant black gang and executed for his former atrocities. The reporters, a man and woman, don't seem to be satisfied with this theory. The woman is a TV newswoman. The host of one of the American propaganda programs we've heard about. The man, however, seems more likely to be a problem."

"Indeed?" Po raised his scant eyebrows.

"N'Cromo says his name is Steve Benson; yet he has been unable to learn any more about his identity. No one seems to know anything about Benson: who he works for, where he comes from, anything."

"He isn't with the television station that employs the woman?"

Chung shook his head. "He seems to be more or less working on his own with only a minimal contact with the TV woman. Perhaps he isn't a reporter?"

"One of our bases is in Chicago," Po remarked, glancing at the map.

"That is why N'Cromo is concerned. The base is a small one, located in a Spanish section of the city and operated by a few Latinos. They've been breeding some sort of insect for future use. I can find out from Doctor Kowdow what those are. Anyway, this man Benson hunted about in the black communities for a day or two and now, according to N'Cromo, he's moved to the Spanish sector."

"I see," Po stated thoughtfully. "Relay a message to N'Cromo and inform him to keep this investigator under surveillance. If he seems to be getting too close to our operation in Chicago, kill him. We can't take any chances that even a portion of Plague Five might be uncovered before we're ready to strike."

"It will be done, comrade colonel," Chung assured his commander.

"All we need are a few more days," Po said, speaking more to himself than his aide. "Then Plague Five will be unleashed upon the Americans and it will be too late for *anyone* to stand in our way."

7

DEAD END SEARCH

"¿Reconoce usted este caballero, señor?" the Penetrator asked the bartender to whom he showed the wallet-sized photograph of Raymond Barr.

The barkeeper studied the picture for a moment and shrugged. *"No, señor."*

"Gracias," Mark Hardin replied with a sigh of disappointment. He rested his elbows on the counter and sipped a mug of beer, mentally reviewing his recent activities.

After he'd left the Arness Clinic with the persistent Penny Gleason, he'd taken the girl to a restaurant, promising to explain who he was and why he'd become involved in the hunt for Raymond Barr. Penny impatiently waited while Mark glanced over the menu and asked her what she'd like. The waiter arrived and Mark gave him their orders. Then he made a show of checking his wristwatch and announced that he had to call his wife. Penny frowned and Mark wondered if it was because she didn't trust him or because she'd learned he was married.

"Hey," the Penetrator replied, shrugging helplessly.

"Even the wife of a federal investigator can't get used to her husband's profession enough to prevent worrying about him from time to time."

"What kind of investigator?" Penny asked, watching Mark rise from his chair.

"I'll tell you when I get back, okay?"

To Mark's overwhelming relief, he located a side exit near the rest rooms and slipped out the door. He felt a twinge of guilt that he'd lied to Penny, but he'd done it for her own good as well as his. At least he'd left a twenty dollar bill under his napkin to pay for the meals.

Escaping from Penny proved to be easier than locating the elusive Raymond Barr. At a loss where to begin, the Penetrator spent four days searching the black and Latino sections of the South Side of Chicago. Grateful for his dark, half-Cheyenne features and the .45 Star PD in shoulder leather beneath a loose-fitting black Windbreaker—only an idiot would wear a suit while roaming the ghettoes and barrios of the Windy City—Mark had visited dozens of bars and pool halls, dropping five dollar bills on counters to get the attention of bartenders and hustlers before he asked them about Raymond Barr. Four days, $200, and about two gallons of beer later, the Penetrator hadn't learned any more about the location of the demented scientist than he'd known at the beginning of the mission.

Sitting on the barstool in El Indulgencia—a two-bit tavern on Market Street that failed to live up to its name, unless one cared to indulge in watered-down booze, dime bags of pot, or $15 junkie-hookers who seldom bathed—the Penetrator was almost inclined to agree with the Chicago PD that Barr had been taken from the asylum and murdered by his abductors. Mark berated himself for such an idea. It didn't make sense. Why had two Latinos been involved in the kidnapping and why hadn't they simply killed Barr at the sanitarium? Of course, the Chi-town cops like nice, easy explanations that require a minimum of investigative effort. That wasn't good enough for the Penetrator . . .

"Hello, Steve," a sweetly caustic voice declared, jerking him from his reflections. "You sure go in for class joints, don't you?"

Mark stifled a groan, then turned to face the speaker. He'd already recognized her voice, but a glance confirmed that it belonged to Penny Gleason. "*No comprendo inglés,*" he muttered.

"Don't give me that shit, Steve," she snapped.

"You shouldn't be here, Penny," he sighed. "This is a rough neighborhood."

"I noticed," the girl commented, climbing onto the stool next to his. "And I figure you're here for the same reason I am. You don't buy the cops' theory about Barr either, do you?"

"Look, Penny," Mark began. "This is my third beer. Let me visit the little boys' room and then—"

"Oh, no you don't!" she vehemently insisted. "You aren't going to sneak out on me again. If you're going to the john, I go along and hold it for you."

"All right," he agreed with exasperation. "Let's talk this over somewhere else."

"Fine." Penny smiled coyly. "I've got a room at a fleabag on Wells Street. Let's go."

Raul Contreras smiled around the stub of a black cheroot when he watched the Penetrator and Penny Gleason emerge from El Indulgencia. "Oh, the *misterioso hombre* and *señorita* television are together again."

Juan Rubio, seated next to Raul in a battered old Ford Galaxy, nodded without enthusiasm. He envied his friend Trini, who had been transferred to a base in New Mexico until he could recover from the gunshot

wound he'd received during the raid on the Hargate
State Hospital. Juan almost wished he'd caught a
bullet in his leg as well. At least Trini was in a nice
warm climate and he didn't have to take orders from
that *negroide* giant N'Cromo.

"So, we follow them, no?" he asked, watching Mark
and Penny climb into the girl's red Pinto.

"*Teniente* N'Cromo does not think that would be
wise," Raul replied. "He says it is all right to follow the
girl, for she is young and inexperienced, but this man
Benson seems too shrewd and competent. That is
why we have had to take great care in tracking his
movements. *El teniente* feels certain Benson is someone special."

"*Sí*," Juan muttered. His partner's admiration for the
africano irritated Juan. "So what do we do now?"

"Since they left in the girl's car, they're probably
going to her place. She rented a room on Wells Street
in a small hotel. Finding them will not be difficult.
Teniente N'Cromo already had planned to dispose of
her tonight. With a bit of luck, we might be able to deal
with them both, no?"

Juan nodded, wishing the entire business was over.
So the Third World wanted to conquer the United
States. Why should he be involved? Juan Rubio didn't
know what they wanted it for in the first place.

Penny's description of the hotel as a "fleabag" proved
most accurate. Her room contained a bed, a chest of
drawers, a black and white television set—chained to
the wall—and a small closet. Although a sink was
included in the furnishings, one had to go down the
hall to use the bathroom or shower.

"Talk about class joints," Mark dryly commented
when they entered the room.

"I'd rather talk about you, Steve," Penny declared,
sitting on the edge of the bed. She crossed one trim,

denim-clad leg over the other and stared up at her guest. "Who are you? What are you?"

"I thought you wanted to discuss Raymond Barr?" the Penetrator remarked.

"That's why I'm in this dump, fella," she confirmed.

"That's not a wise move," he warned her. "Getting a room in a place like this is a good way to wind up a statistic on Chicago's ever-growing crime tally."

"I figured I'd get more cooperation from the local residents if I seemed to be a part of the community." The girl shrugged.

Mark grinned. "You don't fit the role, hon. Even if you spoke fluent Spanish and wore a black wig and brown contacts, you couldn't pull it off. Besides, from what I've been able to gather, it'd be a wasted effort anyway. The folks in the ghettoes and the barrios haven't clammed up about Barr—they simply don't know anything about him."

"How can you be sure?" Penny insisted.

"Because I've dropped enough bucks into the hands of guys who were plenty eager to earn more by telling me what I wanted to know," Mark explained. "I also watched for hints from their body language. Nobody glanced away from me before they replied, no one fidgeted their fingers before shrugging, anything like that. I'm afraid we've both been barking up the wrong figurative tree—again."

"So, what do we do now?"

"*We?*" the Penetrator raised his eyebrows. "Oh, hell. I guess we might as well try to cooperate since we seem destined to keep crossing paths."

"Great." Penny smiled. "You can start by telling me about yourself."

"I can't," he shrugged. "I'm working undercover and I can't afford to reveal anything about myself or who I work for. You'll have to trust me, Penny."

"After you pulled that vanishing act . . ." she growled.

A frown creased her brow. "Hey, are you really married?"

"No," Mark admitted. "How's this," he began. "If you'll agree to stick with the safe leg work and allow me to handle the deeper, dangerous stuff, I'll give you any and all information possible when I find it. You'll have one helluva inside story, and I'll try to save whatever evidence I can for you to film before the police can get their hands on it."

"And an exclusive interview with Doctor Barr—if he's alive—and/or his captors?" Penny asked eagerly.

"Done," the Penetrator agreed.

"Okay, it's a deal."

"Fine," Mark sighed with relief. "How can I get in touch with you in the morning?"

"Oh, no!" Penny produced a gamine smile and added slyly, "I'm not letting you out of my sight, mister."

"You plan to chain me to the bed?" he inquired dryly.

Penny slowly began to unbutton her blouse. "Will that really be necessary, Steve?"

"Not hardly," Mark admitted, feeling the rising swelling in his loins.

NOT FOR RESALE

The Penetrator and Penny Gleason made glorious love for more than an hour before drifting into a pleasantly exhausted slumber. Naked beneath the sheet, Mark was disturbed in his sleep when something tugged at his nostrils. The odor lacked strength enough to rouse him, so he merely stirred slightly and moved closer to the firm, silky-fleshed body of his companion.

Plop.

The sound would have failed to get Mark's attention if his slumber hadn't already been interrupted. His eyes opened wearily and he turned his head toward the sound—which had resembled a drop of water striking the pillow near his head. Figures, he thought, the ceiling leaks.

Then his eyes widened when he focused on the eight-legged, black creature scant inches from his face. Its four eyes seemed to regard the Penetrator with hostility and spindly mandibles twitched angrily as it approached. Mark glimpsed a scarlet patch under the spider's bulbous abdomen.

A black widow! The most poisonous spider in the Western Hemisphere. Mark caught and held his breath before he could utter an involuntary gasp. He tried to remain perfectly still, aware that spiders have severely limited vision. Movement attracts them.

Plop! Plop! Plop!

More of the raindrop sounds puzzled Mark until he carefully shifted his gaze from the black widow to look up at the ceiling out of the corners of his eyes. What he saw sent icy shards of terror bolting up his spine.

Dozens of black, many-legged figures scurried above the bed. Some fell from the ceiling to drop on his and Penny's sheet-covered bodies. Wisps of smoke crept from the cracks that emitted the black widows.

Only the Penetrator's superb self-control prevented him from trembling. He rolled his eyes back at the first spider. It had drawn closer; the tips of its two foremost legs nearly touched Mark's cheek.

His lungs ached from holding his breath while he slowly moved his left hand—the one farthest from the black widow positioned by his head. His heart thudded rapidly inside his chest and the pulse behind his ear increased to a maddening tempo. Mark wondered how many spiders already crept across his body. He seemed to feel them, hear them moving. This had to be his imagination, but his nerves still screamed at him to get out of the bed and away from the black, hairy horrors as fast as possible.

The Penetrator's superb training allowed him to refuse to surrender to this impulse. Gradually, he slid his left hand up his bare chest. Are the fangs of a black widow able to pierce cloth? The thought froze him for an instant. Would movement disturb the creatures that crept across him, separated from his vulnerable flesh by a mere cotton sheet? Mark tried to repress such thoughts as he continued to move his hand and left arm while the rest of his body remained immobile. His fingers touched his breastbone, rose higher to the manubrium, almost to his throat.

Now!

Mark gripped the top of the sheet and thrust his arm forward, snapping the cloth away in a single rapid motion. His whole body moved, shifting away from the spider on the pillow. Instantly, he swung his right arm, bringing the back of his hand down on the black widow and smashing it into a stygian smear with bulging yellow guts at the center.

The Penetrator heard Penny gasp when the violent motion abruptly awakened her. Mark had already bolted from the bed, trying to locate the black, crawling figures that scrambled amid the shadows. He dashed to the light switch.

"Don't move!" he ordered an instant before he hit the switch.

A naked lightbulb overhead flickered on and bathed the room in a harsh, yellow glare. Black widows crept across the floor, rapidly seeking shelter from light. Basically timid, the arachnids were creatures of the dark and generally aggressive only if something entered one's web. A few of the spiders ran into each other and began fiercely fighting among themselves. Others scrambled blindly toward the Penetrator's bare feet. Penny screamed. Four widows were still on the bed and others dropped from the ceiling in a small cascade.

Mark quickly sidestepped the advancing spiders,

which ignored him and ran to the wall in search of a hiding spot. Mark grabbed a shoe, shook it, and sent a black widow tumbling out. Penny shrieked in terror and drew her naked legs close to her body. The girl stared at the hideous arachnids on the mattress.

Terrified of remaining on the bed, she also realized the floor contained more spiders. Petrified by this knowledge, Penny gaped at the living nightmare that surrounded her. Then her eyes rolled upward and a sigh emitted from her parted lips as she fainted.

Mark used the shoe to brush the black widows off the bed. He pulled the unconscious girl closer, noticed a black object creep along her brown locks, and flicked the spider out of Penny's hair with a thumb and fore-finger. The Penetrator gathered her up in his arms and froze when he felt something touch the toes of his right foot. A widow crept onto the upper surface, waited for two heart-stopping seconds, then trotted under the bed. With a sigh of relief, Mark slung Penny over his shoulder and carried her to the door. Opening it, he hauled the girl into the corridor and placed her on the floor.

A quick glance about the hallway assured him her screams hadn't attracted the interest of any of the other tenants of the building. The hotel was located in the type of neighborhood populated by people who were accustomed to loud voices and seldom bothered to get involved. In this case, Mark felt grateful for their apathy. He didn't want to waste any time explaining why he and Penny were in the corridor stark naked.

Braving the spiders once more, the Penetrator entered the room. Most of the black widows had already retreated to the nooks and crannies, but he discovered several of them when he shook his trousers and Windbreaker before pulling them on. Stuffing his wallet and other valuables into the pockets of the jacket, Mark ignored his socks and shirt, grabbing only shoes, the Star PD, and shoulder holster. The only other item he took time to remove from the room was a terry-cloth bathrobe from the closet. After making certain Penny's garment didn't contain any hidden spiders, he draped the robe over its unconscious owner.

The Penetrator couldn't claim to be an expert when it came to spiders, but he knew one thing: arachnids don't start fires. The wisps of smoke he'd seen coming from the cracks in the ceiling told him humans had masterminded the black-widow attack. With shoes and shoulder holster in one hand and his .45 in the other, Mark cautiously ascended the stairwell in search of the kind of vermin he specialized in exterminating— the two-legged variety.

"Do you think the spiders killed them, *teniente?*" Raul Contreras asked the towering African while he stomped the burning cardboard to extinguish the flames.

"I don't intend to try to peek through the cracks to have a look," N'Cromo dryly commented. "I can do without having one of those black widows bite me in the eyeball, and I suggest you just let that fire burn itself out, just in case."

"Oh!" Raul's eyes expanded with alarm. "*¡Sí, Teniente!*"

"Do you think we should go down there and check on those *gringos?*" Juan Rubio inquired, screwing the silencer into the threaded end of the extra-long barrel of his Smith & Wesson Model 59.

"The idea was to avoid gunplay," N'Cromo told him. "After all, a couple of reporters being bitten to death by a nest of spiders might seem bloody odd, but no one is apt to associate it with Raymond Barr. Now, we heard that girl scream. If she attracted any attention, we'll have a devil of a time explaining why we're running down there with firearms, won't we?"

"What if the spiders failed?" Raul asked. "We can't

be certain both of these troublemakers were killed."

"If they survived," N'Cromo began, gathering up his Ithaca riot gun and sliding it into a leather carrying case. "We'll deal with them later, using more conventional methods if necessary. Right now, we have to concentrate on getting out of here undetected."

"*Sí,*" Juan agreed, shoving his silenced pistol into a vinyl AWOL bag. He didn't zip it shut, in case he'd need the Smith & Wesson before they could make good their escape.

"We leave the way we came in, no?" Raul inquired as he inserted his weapon—a .22 caliber Ruger Standard automatic with a full-barrel silencer—into a bag identical to Juan's. "Out the window and down the fire escape?"

"We won't use the bloody stairs, old boy," N'Cromo answered, zipping the shotgun case closed, though leaving the wide end at the buttstock open.

The African wondered if Raul was really so stupid that he needed to ask such a question or if his mind had simply been programed to follow orders to such a degree he was afraid to think for himself. That was the problem with Marxists, no personal initiative.

To be certain, N'Cromo said all the proper rhetoric to keep his superiors and compatriots happy, but he fully realized all the talk about the world's class struggle and international equality to be utter rubbish. Did the Communist leaders in Moscow and Peking live in the same manner as Russian or Chinese peasants? Certainly not! Nor should they, in N'Cromo's opinion. Men were not equal by nature, thus they could not be made so by politics. N'Cromo was seven feet tall and his IQ had been judged to be close to 170. What would Marxism do about that? Could the egalitarians make him shorter and duller, so he could be an equal among men who were his physical and mental inferiors? Rubbish!

Yet, N'Cromo was a Mabiti, a descendant of the great Zulu warriors, the fiercest, best organized, and most highly civilized of black Africans. Despite their discipline and courage, the Zulus hadn't been able to stand against the technology and superior tactics of the British. N'Cromo despised the white race for seizing control of his ancestors' homeland, and he felt contempt for most of his fellow Africans, who docilely accepted *bwana's* domination.

Of course, all that was changing. White rule in the Dark Continent had dwindled rapidly since the beginning of the twentieth century. Only South Africa remained under white-minority rule. Yet, the revolutionaries from Angola to Zimbabwe had not acted alone or without foreign guidance. Russians, Chinese, and Cubans had advised, coordinated, and assisted in the "liberation," and N'Cromo had no doubts that the Communist powers intended to rule over their puppet governments in Africa as they had done in Asia, Eastern Europe, and Latin America.

Since Marxism seemed destined to dominate the continent, it seemed logical to N'Cromo to become a Marxist. Or at least appear to believe their lunacy. A man with his qualities and abilities would not be ignored by the movement's leaders. Indeed, he had risen in the ranks already. In time, he might achieve a position worthy of his superior nature, so he'd continue to play their foolish game until his personal day of glory arrived.

The trio prepared to leave the room. Raul opened the door and stepped into the corridor. Suddenly his midsection exploded in agony. A bare foot drove a powerful karate kick to his lower abdomen, the toes arched back to strike with the hard ball of the foot. Raul doubled up with a gasp and the butt of a pistol hit him behind the ear, knocking the Latino unconscious.

Discovery of the man they knew as Steve Benson

standing before them in the hallway with a gun in his hand startled N'Cromo and Juan Rubio. Both men had been well trained, though, and responded instantly to the threat. Juan's hand dived into the open AWOL bag to grab his 9mm pistol, while N'Cromo swung the shotgun in its sheath like a fighting stave.

The Penetrator saw the long metal tube rise from Juan's bag, immediately recognizing the silencer. The Star automatic in Mark's fist roared and a 185-grain JHP projectile smashed into the center of the Latin's swarthy face. The bullet shattered the bridge of Juan Rubio's nose and sizzled into his brain before popping open the back of his skull like a balloon.

Juan became an instant corpse, propelled backward across the room by the impact of the .45 caliber slug, and falling gracelessly to the floor.

Recoil from the Star PD snapped Mark's gun hand to the right and spared him a broken wrist when N'Cromo swung the barrel of his riot gun. Nevertheless, the blow landed against the slide of the Penetrator's pistol, knocking it from his grasp.

Moving wtih feline speed and well-conditioned reflexes, N'Cromo followed up his attack with a fast butt stroke to his opponent's head. The tactic would have succeeded if the Penetrator hadn't been even faster and better trained than the Zulu.

Mark bent his knees and ducked beneath the sweeping shotgun stock, then he instantly drove a *seiken* punch between the tall man's legs. The big knuckles of the first and second fingers of Mark's fist struck with piston force, literally bursting N'Cromo's testicles. The giant gasped in utter agony, his seven-foot frame paralyzed by unbelievable pain.

The Penetrator rose between N'Cromo's extended arms, pivoted, and seized the shotgun in a single fluid move. N'Cromo still held the weapon tightly in his fists, his grip increased by the tenseness of his muscles after the karate punch to his groin. Mark suddenly dropped to one knee, pulling the dazed African forward to hurtle over his arched back. N'Cromo's shoulder blades slapped the floor, the impact forcing his breath from his lungs.

With a hard twist, Mark wrenched the riot gun from his adversary's weakened grasp. He gripped the scattergun as one might a butter churn and brought the stock down hard. The butt stamped into N'Cromo's throat, turning the thyroid cartilage and windpipe into mush. Blood spewed from the African's mouth. His long body convulsed wildly for a moment before falling limp in acceptance of death.

The Penetrator released a tense sigh of relief and laid down the riot gun to retrieve his Star PD. Aware that the gunshot would alert even the most callous of neighbors, Mark quickly dragged N'Cromo's corpse and the unconscious Raul Contreras into the room. He gathered up his shoes and shoulder rig he'd placed on the floor near the doorframe and kicked Raul's AWOL bag across the threshold before entering and closing the door.

Raul groaned as consciousness gradually returned. Mark put on his shoes and stripped off the Windbreaker to slip the straps of the Alessi rig across his bare torso. He'd donned the jacket once more and yanked up the zipper by the time Raul's eyelids parted.

"Who sent you?" the Penetrator demanded, kicking the Latino in the thigh muscle to rouse him. *"¿Quién los despachó?"*

"I follow orders, *señor,*" Raul replied slowly in his native language, staring up at the black muzzle of the .45 in Mark's fist. "*Teniente* N'Cromo knows more than I."

Determining which man had the African name was simple enough. "Your lieutenant is dead," the Penetrator informed him. "If you don't want to join him, you'll answer my questions. Why did you try to kill *Señorita* Gleason and me?"

Raul listened to the rapid-fire Spanish and replied feebly, scratching at his right shin. "You asked too many questions about Doctor Barr."

"If you're trying to go for a weapon in an ankle holster, forget it," the Penetrator warned. "What about Barr? Do you know where he is?"

"We took him from *el manicomio*," the Latin stated. "He is supposed to help make the chemicals that control *los insectos*."

"Insects?" Mark's brows knitted. "What are you talking about?"

Raul smiled. "*Los Estados Unidos* is going to be reduced to rubble, not with bombs, but insects! Ants, wasps, even termites. Mexico and Canada, too. You can't stop us. Nobody can."

The Penetrator felt a shiver crawl up his spine. That's why he and Penny had been attacked by spiders. He recalled an article he'd read about pheromones years ago. Insects *are* controlled by such chemicals. Could they also be programed to serve as weapons? "Where's your base of operations?" he snapped.

"There isn't *a* base," Raul replied. A wild laugh ripped from his lips. "There are *dozens* of them! You better tell your *gringo* President to surrender right now."

"You bastards must have a headquarters," Mark insisted. "Where is it?"

Without warning, Raul screamed. He suddenly began to slap furiously at his right leg. Two black widows scrambled from his pant cuff. Several of the arachnids had crept into his clothing when he'd tried to stomp out the burning cardboard. Raul had failed to feel the spiders due to the thickness of the hair on his leg, but the creatures had encountered each other and fought, biting Raul several times in the process.

Black widow poison is a neurotoxon, similar to cobra venom, but the amount injected by a single spider's fangs is generally too small to be lethal. However, Raul hadn't been bitten by only one widow. His body thrashed in convulsive fury until his muscles stiffened. Mark leaned forward and looked down at Raul's face. His eyes were open and glassy, although his chest still rose and fell with gasping breaths. Shock, the Penetrator realized. The Latino agent would be in a coma until the venom killed him. Mark opened his Windbreaker and slid the Star into shoulder leather.

"Insects," he muttered in decreasing disbelief.

"What are you talking about, Steve?" Penny's voice inquired from the doorway.

The Penetrator turned to see the girl standing in the open space. He cursed himself for concentrating on his captive and failing to notice the door creak open. Clad in her robe, Penny stared at the trio of bodies on the floor and nearly swooned once again. Mark wished she would, but his luck didn't hold.

"I came to in the hallway," she gasped, leaning against the doorframe. "Then I heard a gunshot. Came up here. Saw blood on the hall floor. Heard voices in Spanish. Must not be thinking straight to just walk in like this . . ." her voice faded.

"You need to rest, Penny," Mark told her, hurrying out of the room.

"Steve," the clarity of her hazel eyes returned as she looked sharply at him. "What's going on?"

"I can't tell you now," the Penetrator answered. He heard the wail of approaching sirens. Time was running out fast. "I have to go, Penny."

"Wait!" she insisted. "I'm going with you."

"Not dressed like that you aren't," Mark grinned, then turned and dashed for the window at the end of the hall. As he'd hoped, there was a fire escape.

"Damn you, Steve!" Penny exclaimed in helpless rage while she watched the Penetrator climb out the open sash. "Shit! Aww, shit!"

8

"YE SHALL BE VISITED BY PLAGUES"

The Penetrator had hoped that Raul Contreras's claims about an insect war had been the ravings of a lunatic, employed by the madmen who had enlisted Dr. Barr in a scheme they were incapable of carrying out. True, Barr was a genius in the field of biochemistry, but nothing in his records revealed any expertise in pheromonal research. Perhaps the entire episode had been a bad dream someone would never turn into reality.

Three days later, the nightmare began.

Enormous swarms of locusts seemed to appear from nowhere in Texas and Oklahoma, swooping down on crops with an almost vengeful hunger. Crop dusters saturated the living clouds with insecticide. The locusts showed no effect from the poison. More than one angry farmer charged into his fields with a spray can full of bug killer or a broom in a futile effort to kill as many pests as possible. The locusts actually *attacked* the humans, swarming over their opponents and biting fiercely. The mouth of the locust is basically designed for chewing; yet it is capable of a painful, pinchlike bite. The insects often succeeded in drawing blood from the farmers who assaulted the unnatural swarms. Seven people had to be hospitalized.

Cases of typhus, bubonic plague, and even malaria began to be reported in various parts of the country. A school in Brownsville, Texas, was invaded by a swarm of murderous bees. Three children were stung to death. The body of an old man, described as "a local wino," was found at the outskirts of Battlefield Park in Vicksburg, Mississippi. His corpse was covered with weltlike stinger wounds. The bizarre incidents continued to occur—ranging from an outbreak of plant virus, carried by leafhoppers, in the Idaho potato crop, to an elderly woman in Montreal who awoke with a scream when dozens of hairy rove beetles attacked her in bed.

The Penetrator suddenly had too many potential enemy targets to investigate and no idea what to look for. Fortunately, Professor Haskins knew someone who could help. He contacted an old friend, Dr. Lawrence Feldhaus, an entomologist at the University of Southern California. Feldhaus dissected several bees and locusts involved in the recent incidents and confirmed that the former were indeed the infamous "Brazilian killer bees" people had been fretting about for years. Most considered the fear of a killer-bee invasion to be exaggerated and a bit silly—until now. Feldhaus also discovered that the bees had been unusually well nourished and healthy specimens, which meant they would breed rapidly and carry plenty of venom in their stingers.

The entomologist's findings on the locusts were more interesting and alarming. He discovered minute traces of various insecticides in the insects. Feldhaus explained that when an insect survives such poisons, it and its offspring often develop an immunity or at least an abnormal resistance to the toxic substances in the future.

"Could these insects have been manipulated through the use of synthetic pheromones?" Professor Haskins inquired.

Feldhaus slipped off his black-framed reading glasses and replied, "Yes, that's theoretically possible, but although pheromones could make them swarm or even attack, one would have to use the proper decibel pitch to make them swoop down on a specific target."

"Decibel pitch?"

"Well, in the case of locusts, the proper sound frequency, amplified to a certain volume, acts like a magnet. It's similar to the musical chirp of crickets or the sharp, shrill mating call of the cicadas. This would be less effective with bees, but some sort of flashing red or blue light might attract them as well."

"Perhaps we can question eyewitnesses and learn if there was a helicopter with such lights or a searchlight or whatever," Haskins wondered aloud.

"No one would have noticed the light," Feldhaus explained. "You see, bees can detect colors that humans can't. They're attracted to various flowers and plants because they see ultraviolet frequencies invisible to the human eye. If this theoretical conspiracy you speak of wanted to attract bees, they'd only need to place a large, pulsating ultraviolet light in the area— in the case of the Brazilian killers, an ordinary light— and the pheromones would do the rest."

Professor Haskins relayed his conversation with Feldhaus to the Penetrator. Since both the bee attack and the locust swarms had occurred in Texas and surrounding states, Mark decided to concentrate his efforts in this area. Thanks to the professor's numerous connections and the Stronghold's marvelous computer, they eventually located a possible headquarters for the insect assaults.

Sensato Unlimited was a small mail-order house with an unusually large row of warehouses in Brownsville. Owned by Ricardo Alverez, a Mexican-American whose association with various leftist organizations had earned the suspicious interest of local, state, and federal authorities in the past, Sensato had seemed to be barely struggling along and ready for bankruptcy until recently.

In the last few months, Alverez had ordered large shipments of high-quality amplifiers, loudspeakers, and sonic projectors. Although Sensato specialized in sound systems, usually low-quality PA units for small factories and amplifiers for discos, the company had never served clients who could afford such excellent merchandise.

When Alverez stocked his warehouses with hundreds of pulsating lights that operated by LTC batteries, everyone assumed he'd decided to add disco lights to his commerce. However, according to Haskins's sources, Sensato Unlimited didn't have any new clients and the new gear was apparently sitting in the warehouses. A computer check confirmed suspicions about the pulsating lights shipped in from New Jersey. There were ultraviolet red and black lights.

The Penetrator finally had a solid lead. Mark flew his Mooney 201 from Chicago to Brownsville and hauled out a special aluminum suitcase filled with weapons. He rented an Oldsmobile Omega and located a hotel. After a shower, a change of clothes, and a blood-rare steak for lunch, Mark felt ready to get to work.

With the benefit of a road map, he found Sensato Unlimited. The headquarters proved to be a tiny shop in downtown Brownsville—near the "Friendship Bridge" into Mexico—no larger than one a barber might own. A sign in the window announced that the place was closed. Mark mentally shrugged. The main office of Sensato didn't concern him nearly as much as the company's warehouses.

He located the main target on a lonely stretch of sand road off U.S. 281. Due to the remote setting, the Penetrator merely drove past the warehouses at reduced speed. Three storage buildings, Mark noted, each of them large enough to serve as a honeymoon cottage for elephants. A smaller structure of steel and Plexiglas stood at the end of the warehouses, probably an office building or a good-sized guard shack. The only unusual item Mark noticed was a heavyset black man wearily patrolling the area with a rifle slung over his shoulder. Nothing really unique about that in Texas. The Penetrator recognized the sentry's weapon, a Mini-14. Good piece. There wasn't any other activity outside the structures, but Mark saw three cars and a pickup parked by the second building. Someone was inside.

Mark drove on and gradually increased speed. He hadn't expected to see much from such a casual surveillance, but at least he knew where the warehouses were and their general construction. Mark would return after dark, prepared for a more serious reconnaissance. And direct action if necessary.

A shadow moved in the night, silently gliding through the darkness. The Penetrator stealthily advanced toward the row of warehouses. He'd been trained in surreptitious infiltration when he was in Counter Intelligence and this ability had been perfected when David Red Eagle sent him to the Cherokee to learn the way of Wind Walker. Dressed in black shirt, pants, and rubber-soled shoes, he was one with the night, invisible in the darkness.

The sentry who patrolled the area didn't suspect he was being stalked by an invader. He neither saw nor heard anything suspicious until a hiss broke the silence and a needlelike projectile struck the back of his neck. The man instantly threw down his rifle and began to flail his arms at the air in a desperate, futile gesture. Within seconds the powerful sedative, in a solution of DMSO, did its work and the guard slumped to the ground unconscious.

Mark Hardin lowered Ava, his specially designed CO_2 dart pistol. The sentry's reaction to the .22 caliber tranquilizer dart puzzled the Penetrator until he realized the man must have mistaken it for an insect sting and expected to be attacked by hundreds of killer bees. Mark cautiously moved closer, watching for other sentries.

He knelt by the senseless guard, noting that he wasn't the same man he'd seen earlier. This sentry was Oriental, a Southeast Asian, Mark surmised from his features. Relieving the sentry of his rifle, the Penetrator frisked him for other weapons, found none, and moved on after applying a set of riot handcuffs.

Mark reached the nearest warehouse unseen and deposited the guard's rifle in a dumpster. The Mini-14 wasn't a bad rifle, but the Penetrator carried enough firepower in weapons better suited to his mission. Besides Ava and his Star PD Mark had a Sidewinder submachine gun attached to a long shoulder sling. He also carried a black ditty bag fastened to his hip that contained magazines for his guns and three white phosphorous grenades.

A ribbon of light from the crack at the bottom of the door warned Mark that the building was occupied. Holding Ava ready in one hand, he turned the knob and slowly opened the door. The Penetrator peered inside to see three men unloading wooden crates. He recognized their merchandise: audio amplifiers and loudspeakers. Then one of the trio raised a two-gallon, clear-plastic jug from a box. It contained a pale, yellowish liquid. Could it be synthetic pheromones?

Suddenly a long-haired Latino happened to glance up from a crate and stare at the door. His mouth opened in startled surprise when he saw the Penetrator. Ava hissed instantly and sent a knockout dart into the man's chest. The olive-skinned Arab beside the Latin managed to snarl something in a language that seemed vaguely familiar to Mark a moment before another .22 sleep dart claimed him as a victim. Both men fell in convulsing lumps on the floor while the third conspirator, a round-faced Vietnamese, dropped the pheromone bottle and reached for a .38 Charter Arms revolver on his hip. Ava hissed twice.

One dart hit the man high in the chest, the sharp sting forcing his body to recoil. The Vietnamese lifted his chin and caught the second dart in the hollow of his throat. Although the projectile wasn't supposed to be lethal, the point punctured Nih Mehn's windpipe. He toppled to the floor and lost consciousness, unaware he would suffocate from his swollen throat.

The Penetrator cautiously stepped around his vanquished opponents, alert for other adversaries. He examined the crates quickly. One label stated that a frequency modulator was contained within the box. Mark nodded with grim satisfaction. He had found the locust-manipulation equipment and several men involved, but his mission was far from over.

After checking the building and finding no one else, he bound the Latino and Arab's hands behind their backs with riot cuffs. Then he moved to the rear exit and carefully opened the door. The first warehouse was connected to the second by a short passage. Beyond that, he discovered five men busily unpacking long glass tubes from cardboard boxes. The ultraviolet lights, the Penetrator realized.

There were too many opponents to deal with, armed only with Ava, with only two rounds left. Mark slid the dart pistol into a hip holster and gathered up the Sidewinder in his right hand. He drew back the cock-

ing knob and shoved the door open with a foot, then
entered the second warehouse.

Ten startled eyes turned to face the intruder only to
stare into the black muzzle of the foot-long McQueen
silencer attached to the stubby barrel of Mark's SMG.

"Freeze!" the Penetrator announced.

Three men followed orders and woodenly raised
their hands in surrender. Another, an Iranian fanatic
who held a frenzied belief in his paradoxical Moslem-
Marxist creed, responded by hurling an oversized
lightbulb at Mark and reaching for a 9mm Star automatic in a shoulder holster. The fifth man, a Syrian
who belonged to Al Fatah, threw himself to the floor
and yanked a .357 Magnum from his belt.

Mark's Sidewinder erupted with a burst, *phut, phut,
phut*. The muffled sound belied the destructive power
of the .45 caliber slugs that spat from the submachine
gun. Three rounds ripped ragged holes in the Iranian
lunatic's chest and kicked his body across the room.
The Penetrator turned to trigger another volley of bullets at the prone figure of Ahmed Mohala. The Al
Fatah devotee's Magnum roared and a 185-grain projectile sizzled past Mark's left ear an instant before he
blasted a trio of .45 rounds into Mohala. The Syrian's
face vanished in a spray of crimson and his head
popped open to spill blood and brains across the floor.

The Penetrator didn't waste time congratulating himself on his marksmanship. The three conspirators that
remained had taken advantage of the distraction to
leap into action.

Miguel Sanchez, a former member of the 23rd September Communist League, had spent most of his
time "fighting for the cause" by distributing propaganda
leaflets in Tijuana. Terrified by gunfire and bloodshed,
he stood rooted to the floor and desperately pulled a
diminutive .25 auto from his pocket. The Sidewinder

coughed harshly and three bullet holes appeared in Sanchez, forming a triangle in his breastbone.

James B'Tala, an Angolan terrorist, had jumped to the cover of a stack of boxes containing light tubes and drawn a .380 AMT Back-up from a pancake holster at the small of his back. Before he could use the tiny stainless-steel automatic, Mark squeezed through to full auto and sprayed the boxes with .45 projectiles. The cardboard and glass bulbs within were inadequate to shield B'Tala. A dozen 185-grain bullets ripped through the African's "cover" and B'Tala fell to the floor, the top of his head transformed into bloody pulp. Quickly the Penetrator changed magazines and turned toward the last terrorist.

Chong Kim, the only survivor of the five Third World agents, had scrambled across the room. Unarmed and panic-stricken, the North Korean decided he had only once chance for survival. He bolted to a wide metal door and quickly turned one of three valves on pipes that extended into the wall. Then he turned and seized the bolt that latched the door. The Penetrator approached Chong, confused by his actions until he saw the Plexiglas window on the opposite side of the door.

The next room contained four wooden beehives, gigantic ones. Hundreds of insects were buzzing angrily within the confines. A sly smile slithered across Chong's flat face.

"I release pheromones," the Korean declared in broken English. "Bees kill. You drop gun. Kick over here. Do quick!"

"The bees will kill you, too, chum," Mark said, trying to determine if the Korean was bluffing.

"You shoot, I die," Chong stated. "What matter bees kill both you and me. Drop gun!"

With a sigh, the Penetrator unslung the Sidewinder and placed it on the floor. Kneeling, he shoved the tubular weapon across the linoleum toward Chong. The Korean released the door latch and reached for the SMG.

Mark's hand dived to the Star PD under his arm. The pistol cleared leather, he instantly thumbed off the safety, and, relying on years of training and pure instinct, snap-aimed. Chong's mouth fell open in horrified surprise. He grabbed the unfamiliar Sidewinder. Time ran out before he could learn how to use it.

The Star bellowed and a .45 round shattered the Korean's sternal notch, sending shards of bone into his heart and lungs. Yet, while the impact of the heavy slug propelled his dying body backward, Chong's right leg swung in a *taekwondo* kick at the door. The edge of his foot hit the bolt and slid it back. The metal partition creaked open as the Korean slumped to the floor.

A tidal wave of furious Brazilian killer bees swarmed into the room, headed for the Penetrator. Mark felt a frozen ice pick of fear stab his spine. The .45 automatic in his fist was powerless to protect him from the murderous minions of flying death. He scrambled to his feet and dashed for the door at the other side of the warehouse.

Bees hovered all around him as he ran. Able to fly at forty miles per hour, the insects soon filled the warehouse. They dove in front of the Penetrator, obscuring his vision like a deadly rainstorm. The tremendous buzzing of the swarm grew terrifying. It increased Mark's desperation and amplified the invincible nature of his inhuman adversaries. They hovered everywhere, their numbers too great to count and every one of them driven by a single impulse—*attack!*

Mark glimpsed the figure of a man in the doorway. He saw the squat, dark-faced Third World agent stare in astonishment and terror a moment before he yanked shut the door. The Penetrator's shoulder hit the metal barrier and he heard the bolt slam into place on the opposite side. It sounded like the lid of his coffin had fallen shut.

Dozens of bees landed on Mark's back, shoulders, and arms. Needles of burning pain lanced his flesh, the stingers piercing skin to inject venom. Absurdly, the Penetrator recalled that a worker bee's stinger is ripped from its body when it attacks and the insect is disarmed and dying after its single sting. Great! Three or four bees couldn't sting him again, though thousands remained to take their place.

Mark flailed his arms at the bees, trying to ward them off long enough to find an avenue of escape. He needed some sort of shelter. Spotting the cardboard boxes that filled most of the storage room, he dove into them. The Penetrator and the containers crashed to the floor. Most of the boxes were empty. He slashed one carton at the swarm with his left hand while the other tried to pull more boxes closer to form a barricade.

His mind raced desperately. What does one do if bees attack? Mark wished Haskins had gotten more information from Feldhaus before he'd embarked on the mission. He recalled that one should keep low, since bees tend to fly upward in an enclosed area.

Mark huddled down and pulled more boxes to form a shield. Stingers still stabbed his hands and one caught him on the left earlobe. What a bizarre way to get one's ears pierced, he thought, surprised by his own weird sense of humor under the circumstances. The bees relentlessly closed in.

Then the Penetrator glanced into the open mouth of a container and saw the shredded packing material inside. His memory sparked a vital piece of information that offered him one chance to save his life. Mark reached into his pocket for a Zippo lighter and prayed that the trick would work in time . . .

9

FLAME AND FURY

Abu Hassid frowned when Ricardo Alverez told him about the intruder inside the warehouse, but the Iranian's lips curled up into a cruel smile once Alverez said he'd locked the invader inside with a swarm of killer bees on the loose.

"Whoever the man is," Hassid mused, stroking his neatly trimmed, pencil-thin mustache, "he found the insects he sought. Ironic, is it not?"

"These warehouses are my property," Alverez whimpered with despair. "If the authorities have traced the bug attacks to me—"

"Every revolution has its risks, comrade," Hassid snapped, "and its casualties. Don't forget that several of our brothers have already paid the ultimate price for our struggle."

"You said there wasn't any way the imperialists could know the bees and locusts were part of a plot—I mean a battle strategy to free the oppressed people of America."

"We've searched the area and found no evidence to suggest more than one man is involved," Hassid shrugged, but his actions concealed his doubts. Only a few nights ago, Lieutenant N'Cromo and two of their best men had been killed in Chicago. Still, one or two incidents proved nothing. Plague Five would succeed.

"But how did he find out about us?" Alverez fretted. "About *me?*"

"You must have made a mistake, comrade," the Iranian replied mildly. "After we learn the identity of the intruder, we'll be able to find out who sent him. Right now, I must report this information to headquarters. I'll take the three men who were rendered unconscious by tranquilizer darts. They need medical attention. The other three will remain here with you to clean up after the bees are finished with our unwelcome guest. See to the disposal of the man's body and the six brave soldiers of liberty he killed. It is a pity we can not give them the hero's funeral they deserve, but their sacrifice will not be forgotten."

"Very well, comrade," Alverez agreed without enthusiasm. He feared that he, too, would become a martyr for the cause—and he strongly suspected that if he died, no one would really give a damn whether he was remembered or not.

"Beekeepers subdue insects with smoke," the Penetrator muttered through clenched teeth while he watched the flame of his lighter dance along a strip of paper from a label to ignite the shreds of packing material inside the box. "Unless my memory has gone to hell, most beekeepers burn scraps of cardboard and grass in a can-shaped bellows. They call this stuff packing grass," he observed, fluffing up the coiled strands. "Sure hope it lives up to its name."

Mark swatted several bees away from his face and ears. The swarm had darted about the warehouse blindly, flying in all directions and striking walls, merely to bounce off angrier than before. The pheromone impulse drove them to attack and they continued to search for a target.

Perhaps a hundred or more found the still-warm bodies of the men Mark had killed. Bees sunk stingers into the unfeeling flesh, unaware their victims were already dead. Hundreds of other insects congregated around the Penetrator, trying to slip past his makeshift barricade and strike.

The strawlike shreds burned rapidly, thanks to some sort of chemical treatment that the National Safety Council should probably look into when they could take time out from testing kid's cap guns to make sure they didn't make too loud a noise. Mark ripped a flap off the box and tossed it into the flames. A thick, pungent smoke soon rose from the fire. The Penetrator ripped more cardboard and added it to the blaze.

"More smoke," he thought out loud. "Can't pile too much on or it'll smother the flames. Don't lose your cool and you come out of this alive."

The Penetrator had considered using the white phosphorous grenades against the bees and vetoed the idea immediately. In a locked building with a solid metal door, that action would be suicidal. He kept feeding cardboard and "grass" to the fire until a dense, gray fog surrounded him.

The swarm began to retreat from the smoke. Dozens of insects suddenly dropped to the floor as though their wings could no longer support them. A few passed through the artificial cloud only to fly awkwardly past their original target, completely disoriented by the smoke. Mark noticed three bees land on his shirtfront. They staggered drunkenly, too weak to use their stingers, then rolled harmlessly off his chest.

The Penetrator coughed harshly. He wasn't immune to the effects of the smoke either, but it had a far more dramatic effect on the swarm. Bees recoiled and darted away from the smoldering fire. Covering his nose and mouth with one hand, Mark watched the insects land on stacks of boxes on the opposite side of the room, forming a living blanket of orange and black. They seemed too exhausted to attack. The bees had been subdued—for the moment. All the Penetrator had to do was find a way to escape before he asphyxiated.

An answer to his problems arrived when the door opened and two bizarre figures entered the warehouse. Dressed in thick canvas coveralls, heavy boots and gloves, and helmets with wire-mesh covers over their faces, the pair could have been visitors from Mars. Both men carried large bellows cans that emitted smoke, which accounted for them not smelling the Penetrator's fire. One also had a pistol in his other hand.

Almost relieved to be facing opponents he could fight with conventional weapons, the Penetrator raised his Star PD and squeezed the trigger. A .45 caliber hollow-point projectile hit the gun-toting "beekeeper" in the chest, left of center. His heart stopped instantly and he fell to the floor like a bag of potatoes shaped into the form of a man. The Star roared once more and a bullet punctured the wire mask of the second "beekeeper" before doing the same to his face and brain.

Mark bolted from his smoky shelter and dashed for the door. Reaching the next room, he kicked the panel shut and slammed the bolt into place. Glancing about the first warehouse, he noticed that only the Vietnamese he'd accidentally shot in the throat with Ava remained. The two men he'd tranquilized were gone. Then the front door opened and another figure in beekeeper's gear entered. The CAR-15 in his fists indicated he was more concerned about human opponents than insects.

The man fumbled with the assault carbine, his thickly gloved hands handling the weapon in a desperate, clumsy manner. Mark pumped two .45 rounds into his adversary before the man could manage to work a finger into the trigger guard of the CAR. The Penetrator jogged forward, seized the carbine, and wrenched it from the dying man's grasp. Mark had only two rounds left in his Star PD. A glimpse at the selector switch told him the CAR-15 was a military-issue weapon, capable of semiauto or full auto. Probably purchased by black-market gun dealers who'd smuggled the weapon out of an air force base. Terrorists wouldn't take the risk of buying a traceable automatic weapon from a gun shop in Texas. Mark might need that firepower. He would rather have his Sidewinder, but he didn't intend to go back into the bees' domain to get it.

When no more opponents appeared, Mark shoved a fresh mag into his Star and holstered it, checked the CAR to be certain it had a round in the chamber, and thumbed the selector switch to full auto. Then he cautiously stepped outside, the assault carbine held ready. Glancing about, he found no one lying in wait for him. The ringing in his ears from the sound of gunshots at close quarters diminished slightly and he heard a faint crackle. At first he thought it might be from the fire he had started inside the warehouse, but a flickering glow at the end of the column of warehouses told him otherwise.

Rushing forward, Mark saw Ricardo Alverez inside the steel and glass office. Flames danced near the Mexican-American as he dumped an armful of folders into the fire. The scene created an eerie effect. Alverez seemed to be burning sacrifices to a pagan god.

Sacrifices, bullshit! The Penetrator thought as he brought the plastic stock of the CAR to his shoulder and aimed at the humanoid shape behind the wide window of the office. *The son of a bitch is destroying his files!*

Mark squeezed the trigger.

The automatic rifle rattled loudly, cartridge casings hopping from its chamber, and orange-jacketed 5.56mm projectiles punched holes through the windowpane and ripped into Ricardo Alverez, breaking his backbone in two places and severing his spinal cord at the base of his neck. The Chicano died before he could utter a scream. His corpse fell against the edge of a small metal desk, twitched twice, and slumped to the floor.

The Penetrator ran to the office shack and kicked in the door. Flames still rose from a metal trash can in the middle of the single room. Mark quickly dumped the contents on the floor and stomped the burning papers. After trampling the fire, he gazed down at the charred remnants with disgust. Alverez must have squirted lighter fluid on the files to assist the blaze. Only a few scraps of paper hadn't been reduced to ashes.

Mark checked the area to be certain none of the conspirators remained, then returned to the office. Since the men he'd previously tranquilized were gone and he'd been forced to kill the others, the Penetrator was back to square one in his search-and-destroy mission unless he could find some clues among the charred records.

He gathered up the scraps and examined them under a gooseneck lamp on the desk. Two of the pieces of paper had nomenclatures and prices for merchandise printed on them. Another read: "*ssippi,*" and "*base*" was legible beneath it. Mark remembered the wino in Vicksburg who'd died from insect stings. The last earned a nod of approval from the Penetrator as he read: "Metairie Base, 579 DuPres."

Professor Amir Sadli frowned while he watched his assistant, Luis Gonzales, spill the contents of an eye-dropper on a small rat in a wire cage. The yellowish liquid dribbled across the rodent's fur and the animal shuffled away in annoyance. Seconds later, the rat began to squeal in agony and convulsed across the cage, scratching and biting at its own body in desperation. Gonzales smiled with sadistic pleasure.

"And this rat didn't even realize it had lice until now," the swarthy Nicaraguan remarked.

"Don't use our pheromones for such nonsense!" Professor Sadli snapped. "Torturing that poor creature is unnecessary and cruel."

Gonzales chuckled. "We're using these chemicals to make the insects attack the *norteamericanos*. We're going to kill thousands, maybe millions, of people—yet you're upset about the well-being of a laboratory rat?"

"We are forced to take action against the oppressors of the West," Sadli, who devoted equal fervor to the Partai Komunis Indonesia and entomology, replied self-righteously. "After we have liberated the downtrodden masses and established universal equality, our research in pheromones will be used to control insects throughout the world. In the new world, both of humanity's struggles will finally come to an end: man's war with himself and his battle with the insect.

"If you say so, comrade," Gonzales agreed with a smug, superior grin. He considered such Utopian ramblings to be nonsense. Every system of government and economics must have its ruling elite and obedient peasants. Luis Gonzales planned to be one of the shepherds, instead of a sheep.

Sadli turned to the large glass terrarium that contained more than five hundred common sewer rats, large brown-and-black rodents that shuffled restlessly about in their container. The terrarium was air-tight to protect Sadli, Gonzales, and their two gun-toting sentries from the deadly bubonic plague carried by the rats' fleas, and oxygen was piped into the cage to keep the animals and their parasites alive.

The plague, Sadli thought, grimly shaking his head.

In the fourteenth century, the Black Death claimed more than 75 million lives. Even with modern medicine and technology, hundreds died annually of epidemics in underdeveloped countries. An outbreak in the United States would be dealt with before the plague could spread beyond the infested areas, but the tactic would serve to demoralize and disorient the Amreican populace. Fear is the terrorist's greatest weapon.

In a smaller container, approximately two thousand *Pediculus humanus* crawled across a thin layer of human hair. The closed-top aquarium appeared to hold nothing but the hirsute carpet because the lice were too tiny to be detected by the unaided eye. Even smaller than the insects themselves, the microorganism *Rickettsia prowazekii* was carried by the lice. The source of another dreaded disease—typhus. Epidemics of typhus were common in the Middle Ages and have continued to claim thousands of lives in the twentieth century. Many victims of the Nazi concentration camps died from typhus. Although Aureomycin effectively treats the disease and improved sanitary conditions have reduced the spread of typhus in modern times, the conspirators planned to use the disease to further disrupt and terrorize the nation they hoped to conquer.

"The things we must do for our cause," Sadli muttered in Indonesian so Gonzales would not understand.

The laboratory door opened. It caused no sudden movement since neither man felt alarmed until he saw the tall figure at the threshold. The man held a pistol in his fist with a nine-inch silencer attached to the barrel.

Gonzales cursed under his breath and reached for a .32 revolver in a belt holster beneath his white lab smock. The Penetrator squeezed the trigger of his Colt Commander. The silenced pistol coughed and a 185-grain JHP round tore a ragged hole in the Nicaraguan's chest. The force of the bullet drove him backward into a wall. Luis Gonzales slumped to the floor as both consciousness and life seeped from his body.

Professor Sadli dashed to a metal desk and yanked open a drawer in a desperate attempt to seize a 9mm H & K automatic. Mark Hardin swung the Commander toward the Indonesian, aimed, and fired. A .45 slug smashed into the corner of Sadli's jawline, drilled an abrupt entrance through the roof of his mouth, and found a resting place in his brain. The entomologist whirled away from the desk and crashed to the floor in a lifeless heap.

The Penetrator lowered his Colt and frowned. He'd hoped to take one of the terrorists alive. Mark saw the army of rats within the terrarium and sighed with relief. Apparently he'd arrived in time to stop another outbreak of plague. Scanning the lab, his eyes located a filing cabinet in a corner of the room. He opened the top drawer and extracted a number of records, quickly leafing through the papers.

"Thank God," he whispered when he read the locations of several other bases and names of agents involved.

Other drawers in the cabinet contained records of experiments and formula information on pheromones. Mark gathered up the files and left the laboratory. At the doorway, he hurled one white phosphorous grenade into the room. The bomb would explode in six seconds in blinding flashes of blue white, splashing burning phosphorous everywhere. The Penetrator dashed from the building, confident that the lab, rats, insects, and the lethal diseases they carried would all be destroyed within a matter of minutes.

Another enemy base had been put out of action, he had at least a partial list of enemy locations, but he realized his mission was far from finished . . .

*   *   *

Dr. Raymond Barr entered Colonel Po's office. "Your aide said you wanted to see me," he stated rather nervously. The longer he worked with Po's people, the less he liked the operation.

"Yes, doctor," the Chinese officer nodded. "I understand you were personally apprehended by the Penetrator after that unfortunate business three years ago."

"The Penetrator?" Barr asked with surprise. "What do you want to know about him for?"

"You're one of the few people who's seen the man up close," Po replied. "What does he look like?"

"Well, he's tall, black hair, a rather dark complexion, and his features appeared to be part Indian," Barr answered. "I only saw him that night at the cemetery beside my wife's grave. I was still a bit irrational at the time and—why are you asking these questions, colonel?"

"A problem has arisen," Po said stiffly. "Someone is interfering with our work. One man seems to have launched a personal war against us. I believe it must be the Penetrator."

"He wouldn't have any reason to oppose us," Barr declared. "Why would he object to our efforts to rid the world of insect pests and—colonel, what's going on here?"

Po smiled. "Don't be alarmed, doctor. Our work is for the benefit of mankind. Surely you realize the Penetrator is a criminal. Your country's own FBI and dozens of police departments have been trying to capture the man for years. His reputation as some sort of modern-day Robin Hood is sheer nonsense, encouraged by the media for the sake of sensationalism. The Penetrator is certainly no crusader for humanity, doctor. He's a dangerous, destructive gangster."

"If the Penetrator is trying to stop us, we'll have to do something to protect ourselves."

"Relax, doctor," Po urged. "Even if he discovers the location of this base, we've got more than ample defenses to deal with him. However, the best defense is a good offense. My men will take care of the Penetrator before he can become a serious threat."

"A lot of people have tried that in the past," Barr remarked. "And the Penetrator is still at large."

"True," Po's crocodile smile expanded again before he continued. "But they didn't have our—resources."

Raymond Barr trembled. He wondered, not for the first time, if he'd become part of some insidious plan disguised as a humanitarian endeavor. Should he hope that the Penetrator would be destroyed before he found Po's base? Or pray that the mysterious one-man army succeeded?

If the pheromonal research was being used for evil, the Penetrator might be the world's only hope for salvation.

10

BATTLE OF VICKSBURG

The Penetrator landed his Mooney 201 in Vicksburg, Mississippi. He began to haul his special-arms case out of the plane when a familiar voice greeted him.

"Need a hand with your luggage, Steve?" Penny Gleason inquired cheerfully.

Mark's startled expression made the girl grin. "I've got a car in the lot. No need to get a cab or a rental.

We've got a few things to talk about, don't we, Steve?"

"There's nothing like meeting old friends in new places," the Penetrator muttered.

A few minutes later they were in her Ford Pinto and headed for downtown Vicksburg. Mark leaned back and stretched his long legs to the extent allowed by the cramped confines of the diminutive car. Their journey seemed a trip backward in time to the antebellum splendor of magnolia-shaded streets and stately, dignified mansions of an earlier era. Here and there, brass plaques announced that this cupola or that widow's walk had been destroyed by Yankee shelling. The effect was that of a city-wide, outdoor museum.

"How'd you figure out I'd be here?" Mark asked, certain he wouldn't like the answer.

"I didn't know you'd show up here," Penny admitted, her eyes never leaving the road while she drove. "But I remembered your comment about insects back at the hotel in Chicago after you killed those three men who sicked the spiders on us. Everybody knows that all hell's broken loose from insects throughout the country. I guessed there might be a connection between what happened that night in the Windy City and what's been going on ever since."

"Like you say, the insect problem has been everywhere," Mark observed. "Why are you here?"

"Figure it out, Steve," she replied. "If that's your real name—and I'm sure it isn't. There are big swarms of locusts and killer bees in Texas. Then a bunch of guys are killed in a warehouse that contains thousands of bees and equipment that could be used to manipulate the bugs. Flint arrowheads were left behind, too. Know what that means, don't you?"

Mark groaned. They rolled past the Confederate Veteran's Memorial, the huge gray figure looking somberly down at them.

"You bet your sweet ass you know," she went on

with certainty. "That's the Penetrator's calling card. He left them at that place near New Orleans a couple days ago, too. Seems it was sort of a breeding ground for rats and bubonic plague and God knows what else. So where have the bugs been acting up that's near Lousiana? I came up with Vicksburg, where that wino was stung to death by fire ants."

"Ants?" the Penetrator raised his eyebrows.

"They recently identified the poison in the guy's blood," Penny explained. "Seems fire ants, which are itty-bitty red bugs, can sting like hell. I didn't know ants had stingers. Most of them don't, but fire ants sure do. That wino must have been stung by about a thousand of the little bastards. Anyway, I figured the Penetrator would head here and sure enough, you did."

"Private plane makes sense," she remarked. "Easier to haul your guns and explosives all over the place. And, if you don't file a flight plan, you're not as traceable as on commercial flights." A sudden thought struck her. "There isn't anything in those cases that'll go *boom* if I hit a pothole, is there?"

"Penny, if you really think I'm the Penetrator, aren't you taking a big chance right now?"

"I doubt it," she replied. "You only kill bad guys. You've never put a bullet in an innocent bystander, and I don't think you'll start now. This is going to be one hell of a story."

The girl pulled her Pinto into a parking lot at the Welford Hotel while Mark desperately thought of some way to talk his way out of the situation. Since Penny elected to remain silent when they left the car and walked to the building, he followed her example. The conversation continued when they entered Penny's room.

"Everything makes sense now," she explained, pacing the floor while she spoke. "The Penetrator caught

Raymond Barr after that sickle-cell anemia business in 1980, so he'd naturally investigate when the doctor disappeared from the funny farm. So, you pop up at the Klan rally. After we had our chat with Nurse Johns, you give me the brush-off and start nosing around the ghettoes and barrios. Then we have our night of heavenly pleasures in bed—you're very good by the way."

"Thank you," Mark answered with a grin. Despite the circumstances, the idea of an an article entitled "I Slept With the Penetrator and He's a Great Lay" amused him.

"Then we got rudely awakened by those black widows and you responded to it like the seasoned veteran of living with danger that you are. They dug a .45 hollow point out of one of the men you killed. I did some checking and found out that's the Penetrator's favorite caliber weapon. Everything that followed after that and your arrival here ties it all up in a neat little package with a bow on top."

"Okay," Mark began. "Let's say you're right. What do you intend to do now?"

"Are you kidding?" She stared at him as though he'd admitted to not knowing who the President of the United States was and asked if she'd please tell him who's running the country these days. "I've got a chance for the biggest story of the year! I'm actually *with* the Penetrator in the middle of his most challenging mission ever. I'll get to see him in action, get his side of the story, learn his secrets . . ."

"Sounds like fun." Mark had started to prowl the room while she rambled on. He stopped and opened a closet and peered inside. He decided it was large enough and the door could be latched from the outside.

"Look, Steve—what's your real name, anyway?"

"Poindexter Doe," the Penetrator replied, taking a terry-cloth sash from Penny's robe, which hung in the closet. "Maybe you've heard of my brother, John."

"Honestly." Penny rolled her eyes toward the ceiling. "You have to realize that you can't keep on doing this crime-crusading bit forever. It's bound to get you killed sooner or later. After we wrap up this insect plot or whatever it is, you can go public. Oh, some of the authorities might make a few hassles, but the public loves the Penetrator and there's no way you could ever get convicted of anything and sent to jail."

"Of course, I'll make this announcement on your news program on Chicago television," Mark dryly observed, pulling a large handkerchief from his pocket.

"Hell," Penny raised her hands in an elaborate gesture. "We'll be able to get a special hour-long program in prime time for something like this. You'll make a mint by writing your memoirs. If Nixon could get his published, you shouldn't have any trouble. There'll be books and a movie and more TV specials about you. Man, you're going to be rich. Meanwhile, I'll be the hottest thing in investigative reporting since Woodward and Bernstein. Barbara Walters, eat your heart out!"

"Stardom, here we come." Mark shrugged. Suddenly, he glared at a wall on the opposite side of the room. "What's that?"

Penny turned sharply to see what he'd noticed and Mark stepped behind her and adroitly swung the handkerchief over her head, drawing it across her open mouth and tying the ends together to form a gag. Penny struggled, mumbling unintelligible curses while he pulled her arms behind her back and tied the girl's wrists together with the sash.

"My pa always told me to watch out for women who want to run a man's life for him," the Penetrator remarked. "Owww!" he added when Penny stomped on his foot.

Mark hauled the girl to the closet and gently shoved her inside. He closed the door and locked it, listening to her muffled complaints and the *thump, thump, thump* of her feet kicking the door.

"Just try to relax," Mark urged. "After I've put a few miles between the two of us, I'll call the hotel and have them get you out. Sorry to do this, Penny, but I can't have you poking around in this business." He grinned when he added, "Besides, I'm too young to retire."

The Penetrator drove Penny's Pinto to the airport. He left it there and flew his Mooney to Tallulah, Arkansas, and rode the nineteen miles back by taxi. He rented a car and started for his destination. Mark parked the rental Volvo half a mile from the old house at the outskirts of Vicksburg, near the National Military Park. The area he now entered was fairly remote, with a long stretch of dirt road that seemed to bisect an ocean of tall, uncared-for grass. Mark felt a certain amount of gratitude that his enemies had chosen such a desolate spot for a base. He didn't like to contend with witnesses or bystanders, to say nothing of the police.

An unseasonably chilly wind swept across the Penetrator's shoulders while he surreptitiously approached the house. The dwelling was an unlikely choice as headquarters for a sophisticated terrorist operation. It better suited the set of a Vincent Price movie. Perhaps that's why the conspirators had chosen it.

Since, according to the list he'd found at Metairie, the Mississippi base was presently quite small and poorly supplied, Mark didn't expect to find any detailed records to assist his research for the remaining enemy posts, nor did he hope to find a member of the conspiracy who ranked high enough to know the location of the main headquarters. This would be a simple mission: search and destroy. Shut down the operation before it had a chance to grow.

The Penetrator carried some ideal tools for destruction. In addition to his Star PD and a trio of WP grenades, he also carried his backup Sidewinder. Possibly the best submachine gun ever made, the compact, sturdy weapon, which could convert from .45 to 9mm, featured a unique rotating magazine that allowed easy around-the-corner firing with either hand, and a patented bolt-and-recoil-spring system that reduced movement to almost nothing. It didn't creep, climb, or recoil when fired—probably the closest thing to a perfect full-auto weapon in the world. Mark checked his weapons and closed in on the house.

Although he concentrated on the job at hand, Mark fleetingly wondered if Dan Griggs at the Justice Department, his only ally within the federal government, had received the copies of the Metairie files. The insect conspiracy was too big for even the Penetrator to handle on his own. Hopefully, Griggs would be able to use the information Mark had sent to motivate the authorities. If the terrorists managed to carry out their scheme to its ultimate, it would be too late to stop them. The insects were too small to be detected and too numerous to destroy. The United States would either be forced to surrender or perish. The Penetrator shook the thought from his mind and crept to the wide, discolored trunk of an old magnolia tree and observed the house, straining his eyes in the darkness.

He saw no movement, no evidence to suggest the shabby, two-story structure was occupied. Had the terrorists learned of his assaults on the bases in Texas and Lousiana and fled to set up their operation elsewhere? Mark carefully worked his way to the rear of the structure, favoring the dense shadows to conceal his movements. A dark green station wagon stood sentry duty by the back porch. The enemy still lurked within his lair. Mark cautiously advanced—unaware of the thin, dark aluminum stalks that extended less than three inches from the ground, concealed by the un-trimmed grass.

The tubelike transmitters were heat sensors that relayed a signal to a receiver inside the house. Joshuah Katanga and Mohammed Khatid trembled when they heard the machine utter three soft beeps.

"One man," Khatid announced, reading the graph that registered body heat of large warm-blooded ani-mals. "He comes from the rear of the house."

"It must be the one they call the Penetrator," Ka-tanga fearfully remarked. "The man we were warned about."

Khatid, a Libyan soldier who'd been recruited for the operation because he'd been unfortunate enough to learn English, picked up a .38 Smith & Wesson revolver and tried to find some comfort in its feel. He failed. Khatid had never been any good with a gun and he'd always been a coward. Now was no time to expect either condition to change.

Katanga's qualifications for heroics were no greater than his partner's. A student of entomology at the University of Nairobi, he knew as much about fighting as a rhinoceros knows about rocket fuel. Both men realized they were no match for the Penetrator. Par-ticularly if they tried to fight him on his terms.

"We discussed what we'd have to do if this oc-curred, Mohammed," the African declared. "We'd bet-ter prepare ourselves and pray that our plan succeeds."

"To what god do we pray?" Khatid inquired bitterly, certain that the Creator would have no reason to look favorably upon men involved in an effort to destroy millions of innocent lives. Was it his imagination, or had the world truly gone insane?

*   *   *

After circling the house to find the best point of entry, the Penetrator selected a partially open window. He checked for alarm wires, found none, and cautiously raised the sash. The easy access to the house bothered him, but the other bases had also featured rather sloppy security and he had no reason to believe the terrorists stationed here would be more careful.

With his Sidewinder held ready, Mark climbed over the windowsill into an unlit hallway. He glanced about the shadow-draped surroundings. The dark lumps of living-room furniture lay like hunchbacked creatures sleeping in the next room. At the other end of the corridor, Mark saw a faint yellow light that served to supply only marginal illumination of an untidy kitchen with a rust-spotted old stove and a sinkful of dirty dishes and cockroaches. The Penetrator approached the soft glow, leary of a trap yet determined to engage the enemy and crush their evil devices.

He entered the kitchen and discovered that the light emitted from an open door that led to the basement. Mark studied the stairs, bathed in a sickly, pale yellow radiance. He took a deep breath and stepped onto the first riser.

Testing each step before putting his full weight on it, Mark descended the steps. Halfway down, he heard liquid splash, followed by the creak of ancient hinges. Resisting an impulse to rush, he cautiously moved to the last tread. The basement smelled musty and was littered with filth. A single bare yellow bulb supplied the only illumination, revealing discarded furniture with broken legs and torn cloth, neglected tools marred by brown rust stains, and a coal bin that contained billows of cobwebs and traces of black dust.

A door slammed at the rear of the cellar.

Mark moved toward the sound. Three stone steps led to a heavy storm door. Someone had escaped.

Yet, Mark saw something that alarmed him far more—a gallon bottle lay on the floor, its yellowish contents forming a wide puddle around it.

Pheromones!

Another pool seemed to form from the shadows. It rippled in scarlet waves and approached the spilled biochemical compound. To the Penetrator's horror, he realized the red ooze did not consist of liquid. Thousands of tiny, living creatures flowed toward him, drawn by the pheromones.

Fire ants!

Mark turned to flee and saw another tide of crimson insects heading toward him. Surrounded. For less than a second he froze, uncertain what action to take. Nature's impulse also seemed most logical under the circumstances. He ran.

The Penetrator dashed for the stairs, trampling across a carpet of fire ants, crushing scores of them. Yet, driven by the undeniable biochemical impulse to protect their colony, the ants continued to swarm toward him. A dozen managed to crawl up his legs, clinging to his pants. Stingers sunk into cloth. A few pierced skin. Venom burned like droplets of acid, forcing a groan of anguish from Mark while he desperately charged up the stairs.

The door had been closed.

Mark grabbed the knob and turned it, although he knew the effort would be futile. Locked. He glanced over his shoulder.

An ocean of red advanced up the stairs. Mark reached into his ditty bag and extracted a white-phosphorous grenade. Holding it in one hand he used the other to aim the Sidewinder at the door and squeeze the trigger.

A three-round burst of .45 slugs splintered wood and shattered the lock case. The Penetrator slammed a shoulder into the flimsy panel and it swung open.

Then he hurled the WP grenade into the basement and bounded into the kitchen. The soft plop of the exploding bomb reached his ears, followed by the *whoosh* of ignited phosphorous. Even the ants couldn't walk through fire to follow him. Mark uttered a sigh of relief . . .

Then he saw the flood of scarlet insects that advanced across the kitchen floor.

11

NATIONAL DISASTER

Fire ants swarmed everywhere.

Millions of them crawled from the kitchen and hallway, all blindly determined to attack the creature that their pheromonal instincts told them endangered their colony. Mark hurled another WP grenade at the insects in the kitchen, realizing his error too late. He might have been able to escape out the back door. The moment he threw the grenade he had committed himself to flee into the hallway or face the hideous death of molten white phosphorous, which eats through flesh and bones like acid through a Dixie cup. Resolute he staggered into the corridor, stomping dozens of ants, while others stung his lower limbs.

When the second grenade exploded behind him, Mark couldn't be certain whether or not some of the WP had splashed him. The insect stings burned so intensely, he wondered if death by phosphorous could be any worse. How much poison did the ants inject with each sting? Mark had suffered half a dozen beestings in the warehouse in Texas. His skin had swollen where he'd been struck and he felt a little woozy for a few hours, though afterward the effects wore off.

The fire ants seemed worse and far more numerous. Every time he tried to swat them away from his body, more would advance, often crawling up his arm. Needles dipped in lava lanced him in a dozen different parts of his anatomy. He'd never experienced such enormous agony.

Mark stumbled toward the window he'd used to enter the house. Someone had closed it. The sill and glass pane writhed with crawling red ants. He recoiled from the window in alarm and fell against the railing of a stairwell leading to the next floor. The Penetrator twisted away from the banister, fearful that it, too, would be teeming with deadly insects. To his surprise, he saw that it was not. In fact, there were no ants on the stairway. The swarm had only been released on the bottom levels of the house. Quickly, the Penetrator bolted to the stairs and mounted them in galloping bounds.

He reached the next floor and hurled his last WP grenade down at the advancing insects. Mark heard the bomb erupt as he jogged along the upstairs hall, slapping at the fire ants that still clung to his body.

Clouds of smoke began to fill the house. The phosphorous had spread rapidly, igniting the old wooden structure into flames. The Penetrator brushed off the last insect that had ridden the "Mark Hardin Express" upstairs and stomped on it. He fell against a wall and inhaled deeply, nearly choking on the smoke. The numerous ant stings had weakened him, though he had to move fast before the fire reached the top floor. At least he didn't have to worry about the ants.

To his nerve-shattering astonishment, Mark saw a column of crimson crawl over the top of the stairs. How could they have survived the blaze below? Sure, they were called *fire* ants, but—then he realized that the insects' pheromonal impulse drove them so completely that they ignored the instinct of self-preservation. Insects don't reason or think, they simply react. The incident, totally macabre, seemed the product of a nightmare.

The Penetrator's mind threatened to slip into unconsciousness, from a combination of the venom in his blood and the gagging gray clouds of smoke. He forced himself to think. He had to get out of the house, and only one hope for survival remained.

He staggered to a door and pushed it open. Mark entered the room, bumping a knee against the brass post of a bed. Blobs of light popped before his eyes and the world seemed to whirl around him as though he stood in the eye of a hurricane. Mark lost his balance and clawed at a wall for support. Cloth ripped and he yanked a thick, rotten old drape from its rod with his grasp.

A window!

Mark's vision cleared and he saw his own reflection in the dusty glass pane. A two-story jump might cost him a broken leg in his feeble condition, though such an injury seemed preferable to the alternatives. The Penetrator seized the sash and hauled up on it.

The frame groaned, jammed, and then rose. Mark crawled across the sill and nearly rammed his head on the thick branch of an oak. Right then, nothing could be so lovely as a tree. He grasped the sturdy bough and hauled himself onto it. Blindly groping, he climbed to another branch and suddenly slipped. Thanks to his superb training, Mark landed on his feet, knees bent to absorb the impact when he hit the ground. He rolled twice and lay on his back, gasping and semiconscious.

"Steve?" a voice called from the other side of the world. "Steve, you're hurt!"

Gazing through a red-misted blur, the Penetrator saw Penny's beautiful face hovering above him. "A good—" he swallowed hard, "investigative reporter has to be observant, huh?"

"Come on," she urged. "Let me help you."

He offered no argument. Penny dragged him to his feet and wrapped his arm around her shoulders. Mark tried to walk on his own, but he leaned heavily against the girl. She was panting from the exertion by the time they reached her Pinto.

At last the Penetrator awoke. His groggy mind tried to recall what had happened in the last twenty-four hours. He remembered the horrendous experience with the fire ants at the old house, but after Penny arrived, everything seemed to get blurry. Mark opened his eyes and saw the girl seated beside him. He then realized he was clad only in his undershorts, lying in a bed in Penny's hotel room.

"How long have I been out?" he inquired, his throat raw and dry.

"You haven't been anywhere," the girl teased. "You've been right here, sleeping for the last six hours."

"Where are my weapons?"

"First thing you'd think of, huh?" Penny sighed. "Most people would want to know if they were going to die or not after getting stung by about a hundred fire ants, but you're concerned about your guns. I locked them in the trunk of my car. Didn't think it'd be a good idea to bring them through the lobby of the hotel. I had enough trouble hauling you in. The clerk probably figures I'm a hooker and I got you drunk to take advantage of you."

Mark tried to sit up. His head spun and he decided not to push his luck. "How'd you get out of the closet?"

"My cosmetics case was in there, which gave me a nail file. I managed to get it out, picked the knots of the sash you tied me up with, and then I slipped the lock with it. Pretty good, huh?"

"You're full of surprises," the Penetrator admitted. "How'd you happen to find me?"

"First I had to find my car, which was where I thought I'd catch up with you. Pretty cute trick, moving your airplane like that. After that, I figured you'd probably go somewhere near where the wino's corpse was found. So I drove around the Military Park area on the chance I might come across you. When I saw a house on fire, I headed toward it and there you were. Just lucky, I guess."

"So was I," Mark observed. "Thank you."

"I should have left you there after the way you locked me in that closet," she said with false severity.

He noticed a number of bandages wrapped around his arms, legs, and torso. "Did you do this?"

Penny nodded. "I used to be a nurse's aide a few years ago. I treated those insect stings with ointment before I wrapped them. It won't do much for the pustules that are going to form where you were bitten. You can drain those and they're full in a matter of minutes. They'll itch like hell, too, for about three days. Also, before I left Chicago, one of my police friends put me in touch with a toxicologist who gave me a vial of antivenom for fire-ant poison after I told him I was coming to Mississippi to investigate the most recent insect victim. Guess who I gave the injection to while he rested after his mighty battle with the bugs?"

Mark smiled. "You're really something, Penny. I'm not just grateful, I'm downright impressed."

"Well," she shrugged sheepishly. "I sort of made an ass of myself when I talked about you retiring as the Penetrator and going public. That'd be a good way to get you killed, wouldn't it?"

"I don't know if I'd call it a 'good way,' but that's probably what would happen."

"Too bad," the girl said with a sigh. "I'd hoped to get a hell of a story, but I'm not going to sacrifice you for it."

"Maybe you can still get a good story," Mark told her. He admired the young TV anchorwoman. She not only had determination and intelligence, she had integrity as well. That was a rare trait among media people. It wasn't very common anywhere else either, Mark thought. "Maybe we can make a deal. You can join me on my next strike, but you'll keep at a safe distance. You've got to promise that. I don't want to have to worry about anybody but myself in a battle. You'd only be a distraction if you get too close and you'll probably get us both killed that way. Understand?"

"Sure, Steve," Penny agreed. "Whatever you say. You're the boss."

"I'll bet," the Penetrator grumbled.

Colonel Po and his aide, Lieutenant Chung, stepped from the colonel's office. Both men strode urgently through the corridor and spoke as they walked.

"Are they certain it was the same man?" Po inquired, buckling his gun belt.

"There's no doubt, comrade colonel," Chung assured him. "That meddlesome Penetrator has at least gone to his ancestors or whatever foolish religious nonsense the Americans endorse. The two men stationed in that province—the one that starts with an *M* and has all those *s*'s and *p*'s in it—reported that they'd trapped the Penetrator in the cellar and released a giant colony of approximately two million fire ants."

"Po!" a voice shouted from behind the pair.

They turned to see an angry Dr. Raymond Barr stomp toward them. "Yes, doctor?" the colonel asked mildly. "Is something wrong? You seem disturbed."

"I overheard some of your men talking about their glorious mission against Western imperialism," Barr declared, his eyes boring into Po's face.

The colonel folded his arms on his chest. "Eavesdropping is impolite, doctor. It can even be unhealthy."

"I understand enough Spanish to realize they were Sandinistan troops, discussing the overthrow of my country!" Barr's expression contorted with fury. "You've been using me in a goddamn Communist plot to conquer the United States with insects!"

Po smiled. "And we really appreciate your help, doctor."

"You—" Barr mentally groped for words, "fucking— bastards!"

Suddenly he lunged at Po, hands aimed at the colonel's throat. Po's arms unfolded quickly and the heels of his palms easily deflected Barr's clumsy attack. Bending at the knees, Po swung the front of his right elbow into the doctor's solar plexus, followed by a knifehand slash to the ribs. Barr flew into a wall and slumped to his knees in a gasping heap. Chung stepped forward and kicked Barr in the chest. The doctor sprawled on his back, sobbing in pain and futile outrage. The lieutenant drew back his foot to launch another kick.

"That's enough," Po commanded. "Our American friend may reconsider his patriotic foolishness and realize his only hope will be to continue to support our efforts. See to it that he's always under guard from this moment on."

"Yes, comrade colonel," Chung rapped in reply.

"With the Penetrator out of the way, we no longer have to contend with any serious obstacles," Po declared. "In less than a week, the United States will be helpless. Within two months, the entire Western Hemisphere will fall into our hands."

*   *   *

Unknown to Colonel Po, opposition to his scheme poised on the verge of escalation. The copies of the Metairie files the Penetrator sent to Dan Griggs soon alerted federal and state authorities to the insect conspiracy. Armed with a list of enemy bases and foreign agents involved in the plot, raids were organized by everyone from the Treasury Department to local chapters of the *posse comitatus*. A dozen bases were destroyed and more than a score of terrorists apprehended. Many others were killed. Unfortunately, the captives proved to be small fry who knew remarkably little about Operation Plague Five. The Marxist mentality is notoriously sheeplike and utterly paranoid. We do this for the great cause of universal equality, they cry. Why are they doing this? Because a wise leader who speaks well and promises Utopia tells them they must. Such zealots need no other justification for their actions. The obsessive fear of discovery on the part of their masters keeps the lower echelon uninformed on nearly everything. The Metairie list was far from complete, and the Third World agents realized the risk of keeping records that might be used to locate other bases.

When raids occurred, the terrorists tended to immediately destroy what files existed. Other enemy posts changed their location and disappeared into the vast countryside. Dozens still remained and swarms of insects continued to spread death and destruction. The odds were still in the terrorists' favor.

Wisely, the Penetrator had purposely left one enemy outpost from the list he'd sent to Dan Griggs. The terororists had an exceptionally large operation in the desert of New Mexico. Judging from the equipment being delivered there and the pheromones, insects, and agents being sent from it, the New Mexican base promised to be the biggest in the United States. Yet, the Penetrator did not believe the actual headquarters of the conspiracy was located there, or elsewhere in the United States. Leaders seldom expose themselves in battle. Since the enemy consisted of a combination of Third World representatives and the bulk of their activity seemed to be in the southern states, Mark surmised that the main base must be somewhere in South America. The most likely source for confirming this information appeared to be in New Mexico.

The Penetrator hadn't kept this data from the authorities because he wanted to grand-slam and prove he could succeed where governments would fail. The fate of the country was at stake and Mark wouldn't take any chances that a clumsy raid might alert the agents at the New Mexico base in time for them to burn their files. He also wanted to lull the enemy into a false sense of security before he made the hit.

Besides, government agencies are subject to information leaks, and if Mark was right about the Plague Five headquarters being located in a foreign country, Washington would try to handle the matter through diplomacy instead of direct action. Only the latter response could hope to stop the evil scheme in time, the Penetrator believed.

Mark regretted his promise to Penny Gleason that she could accompany him on the raid. Before they left, he reminded her that this agreement was based on her staying out of the line of fire. The girl assured him she would. She had acquired a good camera with both a telephoto and zoom lens. Reluctantly, the Penetrator flew to the Southwest with his passenger and a variety of unusual weapons.

The enemy base consisted of four buildings made of joined panels of sheet aluminum, with a few Plexiglas windows. A handful of men could snap everything together in a few hours. A number of large waferlike objects were mounted to the roof of each structure. Photovoltaic cells had been set up to utilize solar power to produce electricity for the site. Two sentries, armed with automatic weapons, patrolled the area, unaware of the keen pair of eyes that watched them through the powerful lenses of Bushnell Armored 8 x 30s.

The Penetrator lowered the binoculars and descended the rock formation half a mile from the base. Penny waited for him by a jeep. Mark told her what he'd seen.

"They've got a nice setup here," he explained. "The location is remote and they can do just about anything they want without fear of detection. Luckily, they don't seem too worried about security. Only two guards."

"What do you think they have in those buildings?" Penny asked, a trace of fear in her voice. "More of those awful bugs?"

"Could be," Mark replied. "But my guess is they're using it basically as a command center for other operations and maybe to produce more pheromones. I won't know until I go down there and give it a look tonight."

"You're really going to do this on your own?" Penny challenged. It didn't sound like a question.

"That's the way I work and you knew it before we came here," the Penetrator reminded her. "It'll be dark in a couple of hours. You'd better get that camera ready. Remember to stay at a safe distance and *don't* take any pictures of me when I'm facing the lens."

"I gave you my word that I wouldn't," Penny protested, her voice revealing hurt at his apparent lack of trust.

"I know you'll keep your word, hon," Mark spoke softly. "Now, let's get to work."

Penny nodded. She glanced at the sun, which slowly descended toward the horizon, a fat, bloated orange baloon. She trembled, aware that the approaching darkness would bring violence and death.

12

DEATH OF AN ANCHOR

Jabari Heykel gazed up at the night sky and smiled. He liked the desert. Jabari had been born to a desert tribe of Bedouins in Egypt. Nomadic, the Bedouins had traveled the ancient sands on their camels and mules and tended to their small herds of goats. They made camp where they wished and moved when they desired to. The Bedouins lived as they had for centuries, their World War II–vintage firearms the only recognition of a changing world, which they chose to ignore. They were free.

When the tanks and planes again filled the desert, the Bedouins were astonished. Europeans had fought in their land before, but those wars had ended years ago. Who fought now and why? Explosions do not care who they kill and the tribe fell victim to the bombs and shells on the fringes of the battlefield. Five-year-old Jabari had been one of the few survivors. His parents, elder brother, and infant sister all died in the carnage.

Afterward, the Egyptian soldiers found Jabari and four other Bedouins, all that remained of the tribe. They took Jabari to Cairo, where he was told the "official" version that the Jews had declared war on Egypt and they had been responsible for the slaughter of the Bedouins, including Jabari's family. Thus, the boy who'd known only the desert and a simple, if harsh, life of wandering learned to hate Israel and that nation's great ally, the United States.

Jabari was a young soldier, not yet in his twentieth year of life, when President Sadat went to Tel Aviv to talk peace with the Israelis. Jabari was outraged by this action. His purpose in life had been fueled and motivated by hatred for the Jewish butchers of his family. Jabari had never considered the fact that Egyptian bombs and shells could just as likely have been the cause of the Bedouins' massacre. If the Egyptian government could offer friendship to the murderers of his tribe, then Egyptians were not his people. Jabari defected to Libya.

Quaddafi's regime proved more to Jabari's liking. He applauded Libya's stand against Israel and the alliance with the PLO, and wept with joy when that traitor Sadat fell under the bullets of Libyan assassins. When Jabari was offered an opportunity to help his brothers of the Third World destroy the United States— that great, rich ally of the Jews—he eagerly accepted and soon found himself assigned to New Mexico as an enforcer for Operation Plague Five.

The station suited the young zealot, for he was once again in an environment that would always be his home: the desert. Jabari stared in appreciation at the stars in the clear, velvet sky. Night in the desert, any desert, was the most beautiful sight in the world.

Then a sharp edge of heavy steel struck the back of his neck. The blade cleaved through the third and fourth vertebra and severed his spinal cord in a single blow. Jabari Heykel, whose life had been ruled by hatred, died with thoughts of beauty and love for the desert before his mind flickered into oblivion.

The Penetrator cleaned off the blood and returned his Bowie-Axe to its sheath. He knelt by the youth to place two fingers to Jabari's neck. There was no pulse. Grimly satisfied that he'd dispatched the first sentry quietly and quickly, Mark crept away in search of the second guard.

He found the man at the rear of one of the buildings. The sentry had placed his twelve-gauge Winchester shotgun against one of the aluminum walls to relieve himself. The man was still urinating, holding his penis in his left hand, as required by Moslem law, when Mark stealthfully approached from behind. The Penetrator drew his Bowie-Axe and swung the big knife once again. Another sentry fell lifeless to the ground.

Mark resisted a sigh of relief. Thus far, his assault had gone smoothly, but he'd only completed the first phase. Speed would be as important as stealth and cunning. Since he had no way of knowing when the guards changed shifts or if a supervisor would check on the sentries, the Penetrator had to act fast.

Running in a low crouch, Mark dashed to a cluster of boulders outside the perimeter of the enemy camp to reclaim the special equipment hidden there. His Sidewinder and a black ditty bag filled with WP grenades were common enough gear for the Penetrator, but he'd also brought half a dozen cannisters of tear gas—which affects most insects more dramatically than it does human beings—a gas mask, and a flame-thrower with two 3-gallon tanks of premix fuel. Mark already carried his Star PD and Bowie-Axe, which completed his equipment.

The Penetrator slipped into the harness of the flame-thrower and hauled the matte-black, camouflaged metal tanks onto his back. He didn't like carrying such a contraption. Bulky, cumbersome weapons had never been the Penetrator's style; yet fire was the most effective insecticide of all time and Mark didn't intend to be caught unprepared if he found himself face to face with another swarm of bees, ants, or any other deadly species housed in the buildings of the enemy camp.

Although in superb physical condition, Mark was breathing heavily by the time he returned to the heart of the base. Tension contributed to the burden he carried. He moved slowly to a door at the side of the first building. There was no light visible in the nearest Plexiglas window. The lock proved to be a simple button-latch type. Mark prayed this meant no alarm system had been wired to the door. He inserted the blade of his Bowie-Axe and expertly sprung the lock.

Mark entered the building and closed the door. He extracted a penlight from a pocket and flicked it on to examine his surroundings. A storage room.

Wooden racks extended from the yellow tile floor to the ceiling. They contained hundreds of five-gallon plastic bottles filled with yellow liquid pheromones. The Penetrator found another door that led to the next room, a laboratory.

Three large metal stills suggested it was either a processing center for pheromones or the conspirators were brewing moonshine on the side. Mark moved to the opposite wall and listened at a crack in the door. He heard two voices conversing in an odd combination of broken French and Arabic, with an occasional word of English thrown in.

Slowly, Mark turned the knob and gradually opened the portal wide enough to peek into the room. Two men, a wiry, hawk-faced Arab and a stout, bull-necked black African, sat at a card table, playing chess and drinking coffee. A shortwave radio set in one corner of the room indicated a probable reason for their presence. The Penetrator poked the bulbous silencer at the end of his Sidewinder through the doorway.

"Que?" the Arab frowned when he saw something move. His eyes expanded when he recognized the thick, sausage shape of a silencer. *"Là!"*

The Sidewinder coughed and three .45 caliber bullets split the Arab's face, kicked out the back of his head, and sent his corpse to the floor. The African jumped from his seat and clawed at a sidearm in a button-flap holster in an instant before the Penetrator's next three-round burst bit into the man's chest and ripped his heart and lungs into pulp. Mark checked the room and found no one else present. He glanced at the bodies of the terrorists he'd slain and wondered how many more would die before the nightmare of Plague Five came to an end—one way or another.

Penny Gleason positioned herself at the cluster of boulders and mounted the Ariflex movie camera, loaded with infrared film and equipped with a telephoto lens, over the top of a rock. The girl nodded to herself with satisfaction. Sure, she'd promised Steve, or whatever his name was, that she'd stay close to the jeep three hundred yards from the enemy base. Nuts! Even with the telephoto lens she could hardly see a damn thing with the camera, let alone expect to film anything worthwhile. Now she had worked her way within fifty yards of the enemy station. Maybe that was dangerously close, she realized, but the boulders could serve as a shield if anything happened. Besides, one can't expect to get an earth-shaking news story about the Penetrator without taking a few risks.

Mark moved to another building and entered it to discover the place contained literally millions of insects, housed in huge glass terrariums. The spectacle would have been more frightening if most of the creatures weren't inactive after dark. Yet, the dozens of beehives, massive paper-and-mud hornet's nests, and ant mounts were disturbing enough. Of course, some species of insects were most active after dark.

Mark grimaced with disgust when he saw a cage filled with thousands of cockroaches. The loathsome insects scrambled about the interior of their container,

NOT FOR RESALE

crawling up the glass walls and over each other, desperately trying to squeeze under the cover of a thick pile of rotten wood. The Penetrator located several terrariums full of spiders, scorpions, flies, and other species, many of which he failed to recognize. It was definitely the most fearsome army he'd ever laid eyes on. The skin on his back crawled when he thought that the insects at this base were only a tiny portion of Plague Five. The Penetrator left the breeding compound and headed for the third building.

It proved to be identical to the one he'd left. More insects. More inhuman soldiers being prepared for the most insidious invasion of all time. He headed for the fourth and final structure, jimmied the latch with his knife, and peered inside.

A shaft of moonlight slithered through the crack between the door and its frame. The light fell directly on the face of a man who lay sleeping on a metal-framed bunk.

The terrorist's eyes opened and he emitted a startled gasp when he saw someone at the entrance. Mark's Sidewinder fired three muffled rounds into the man, punching bullet holes through the blanket to pierce the man's chest and grant him the sleep of eternity. Unfortunately, the terrorist cried out before he died and a dozen voices shouted in alarm.

"Shit!" the Penetrator hissed with self-disgust. "That alerted the whole barracks."

He quickly yanked a tear-gas canister from his belt, pulled the pin, tossed it into the room, and closed the door. Then he ran to the end of the corridor and crouched at the corner. Moments later, men spilled out, firing an assortment of weapons in all directions while they coughed and mopped hands at their burning eyeballs. Mark aimed his Sidewinder and fired. Bodies fell like tenpins to a bowling ball. More men emerged. The Penetrator threw another tear-gas gre-

NOT FOR RESALE

nade and emptied his magazine into the disabled terrorists.

Mark slid to the cover of the intersecting corridor wall and hastily donned his gas mask. Before he could reload the Sidewinder, a figure appeared at the opposite corner, a revolver in his fist.

The Penetrator reacted instantly, ruthlessly, to the threat. His hand hit the nozzle of the flamethrower and a jet of yellow fire shot into the would-be assailant's face. The man screamed and dropped his gun to claw hopelessly at his charred features and still-burning hair. Burned-out lungs terminated the terrorist's agony in a fraction of a second.

Assuming there were more opponents on the opposite side of the building, Mark poked the nozzle of the flamethrower around the corner and opened fire.

Voices screamed in fear and agony. Mark saw a flame-drenched figure stumble and fall while another man leaped to a door, fire dancing on his shirt sleeve. The Penetrator swapped magazines and cocked his Sidewinder. What's next? he thought.

If he remained in his present position, the enemy could easily trap him or kill him. Since they could attack from both hallways simultaneously, all they'd have to do would be to lob a few grenades in his direction. He had to act before they could get their wits together and attack in a coordinated manner. He hurled a WP grenade at the "back door," where the adversaries had already gotten a taste of the flamethrower. Burning phosphorous splashed the wall and surrounding area.

That ought to keep them indoors for a while, he thought as he bolted from his position and dashed for the "front door," where he'd filled the barracks with tear gas. He almost tripped over a corpse, managed to keep his balance, and came face to face with an Oriental terrorist who was vomiting too hard to use the

H & K 53 machine pistol in his grasp. Mark blasted a three-round burst into the man's chest and bounded across the threshold of the barracks building.

He quickly scanned the dense, smoke-filled interior and discovered a lone figure cowered in a corner. The man wore only a pair of boxer shorts and a tattered undershirt. A thick bandage on his thigh revealed why he hadn't fled the building. Coughing violently, Trini Alvedo tried to cover his nose and mouth with his undershirt while he stared up at the awesome creature that threatened to destroy him.

The invader seemed to be nine feet tall, taller even than that accursed *Teniente* N'Cromo, who'd led them on the mission to abduct Raymond Barr. Yet far worse than its size, the beast that stood above Trini did not appear to be human. Its back was black and humped like a fighting bull and its face resembled a hog's snout with two great bug-eyes. *El Diablo* himself had come for him! Trini closed his tear-filled eyes and tried to remember the prayers he'd learned as a youth before he rejected Catholicism for Marxism. A long-dead German socialist couldn't help him now, but maybe God existed after all and perhaps—

Mark Hardin's hand lashed out, the hard edge striking Trini behind the right ear. The terrorist slumped to the floor, almost grateful when his mind dissolved into a realm of unconsciousness.

The sound of an automatic weapon's metallic chatter drew the Penetrator to the doorway. He gazed outside to see two men standing at the front of the building. One, a black man, cradled a badly burned arm with his other limb, a big automatic pistol in his fist. He watched in disgust while his comrade, a slender, swarthy man with a dapper mustache, fired a Smith & Wesson M-76 machine gun into the prone figure that lay a few yards beyond the perimeter. With a sick, sinking feeling, Mark recognized the gunman's victim as the burst of 9mm bullets kicked the body across the sand. A fancy movie camera flew from the corpse's grasp as it rolled from the impact.

"Penny!" Mark cried in anguished horror.

He leaped from the barracks, his mind twisted by outrage.

Abu Hassid turned to see the vengeful figure of the Penetrator. He began to raise his Smith & Wesson chatterbox, but Mark was faster.

The Penetrator aimed the nozzle of the flamethrower and fired before the Iranian could squeeze the trigger. A long, roaring tongue of fire struck Hassid in the legs. He screamed and threw away his smoking M-76. Before he could fall, liquid fire jetted from the flamethrower again and struck him full in the chest.

Hassid's clothing ignited and the hungry blaze ate through to the flesh, gnawing on to touch bone. Hassid shrieked and staggered backward, his body shrouded in merciless flames. Another gush spurted from the bulbous nozzle and struck him in the face.

The conflagration tore into his skin, burned his hair, and melted his eyeballs into slimy, bubbling goo that oozed from charred sockets. Hassid collapsed in a smoldering heap. A final burst of fire from Mark's flamethrower consumed the Iranian's twitching body and forced a terminal wail from Hassid. Flame entered the man's mouth and traveled into his throat, burning his windpipe and filling his lungs with charred debris.

Horrified, the African dropped his pistol and raised his arms to surrender. The Penetrator advanced slowly, the nozzle of the flamethrower pointed at the last member of the terrorist group.

"Not that way," the black man begged, tilting his head toward the burning remains of Abu Hassid. "Please, mon, not that way!"

Mark Hardin nodded. He hadn't another igniter charge in the nozzle anyway, so he let it drop to the side and unsheathed his Star PD. The African actually felt gratitude when the .45 bullets crashed into his chest.

Trini Alvedo groaned softly as he regained consciousness. Weakly, he opened his eyes. Something splashed liquid into his burning orbs and he moaned as the fluid connected with his tear-gas-raw pupils. Trini blinked and his vision cleared enough to see the tall, stern-faced figure who stood before him with an eyedropper in his fist. Trini wondered if it was a doctor.

"Buenos días," the Penetrator greeted, addressing Trini in fluent Spanish. "I regret that I have not prepared breakfast. Instead, I have prepared you to be breakfast for our *amigos.*"

Trini failed to understand his abductor's words. His senses slowly returned and he realized he'd been bound, wrists connected together and ankles fastened by some kind of hard plastic strips. The man's comment seemed meaningless until Trini saw the plastic bottle at the Penetrator's feet.

"That's right, *pendejo,*" Mark said in a mocking voice. "I inserted some pheromones in your eyes. Oh, I killed all of your noble comrades and burned the breeding sectors of insects first, but I saved a couple of bottles of this biochemical witch's brew. The one I chose for you belongs to the family *diptera.* You know what that means, *cabrón*? It refers to *las moscas,* *¿comprende?*'

"The flies?" Trini's eyebrows knitted with confusion. Then he heard the angry buzz of numerous insects. He vaguely became aware of his surroundings. He was no longer in the barracks; the sky above held the pale pink color of dawn. Tall grass jutted between Trini's bound legs and the smell of manure assaulted his nostrils. He'd been transported to a field.

"Look over there," the Penetrator told him, pointing toward a pile of cow dung.

Trini stared in horror at half a dozen large, black horseflies that clustered together on the animal filth. "Noooo!" he moaned helplessly.

"You've figured it out, eh? Smart little fucker, aren't you?" Mark chuckled, a wicked sound. "That's right, *hijo de la chingada,* the flies will soon find you. Have you ever seen how a horsefly can draw blood from an animal's hide? Close your eyes if you want. It won't matter. The insects will bite through the lids and suck your eyeballs until they shrivel up in their sockets."

"No!" Trini cried. "I beg you, *Señor.*"

"But you are a brave soldier of the cause," the Penetrator sneered. "You will gladly sacrifice for your beliefs, *¿verdad?* When the new order takes over, I'm certain they'll give you a medal and a white cane, maybe even a Seeing Eye dog."

"What do you want of me?" Trini sobbed, turning his head away from the horseflies, desperately hoping the insects wouldn't be drawn to the pheromones before he could convince his captor to take him away from them.

"Where's the headquarters for your organization?"

"I don't know."

The Penetrator leered at him. *"Buzzzz!"*

"Nicaragua," Trini replied quickly.

The answer made sense. A Marxist country in Central America fitted everything Mark had already theorized about the terrorists' setup. "Are you certain?"

"*Sí, sí.* Nicaragua is my homeland. The Sandinistans recruited me long ago. Although I have never been to the research center, I know it is somewhere in the north of my country."

"The Sandinistans aren't capable of an operation of this scope," the Penetrator declared. "And there are too many Arabs, Orientals, and black Africans involved. Who's the real brains behind the plot? The Russians?"

Trini's eyes grew round and he shook his head. "No,

the Soviets knew nothing about our plans. They would be furious if they did. We didn't let the *cubanos* know either. Even Castro admits his country is ruled by Moscow. No. The Chinese are responsible. Our leader is a *Coronel* Po."

"Colonel Po?" Mark's eyebrows rose. "Po Hahn Chau?"

"*Sí*. Something like that," Trini nodded weakly. "Who knows about such strange names?"

"That's one name I'm not likely to forget," the Penetrator stated in a cold voice.

Mark Hardin bitterly recalled a special mission he'd undertaken more than a decade ago. During his first tour in Vietnam, intelligence learned the location of Colonel Po's infamous POW camp near Hanoi. They had organized a Bright Light team, including Sergeant Hardin, to coordinate with Toro Baldwin's Fifth Special Forces people. The assignment: to assassinate the Chinese butcher. Unfortunately, when the hit squad reached the camp, Po had already been called back to Peking.

Now Mark vowed to rectify his earlier failure, though he warned himself not to allow his emotions to interfere with the immediate mission. His anger at Penny's death had caused him to kill two men whom he might otherwise have captured for interrogation. No matter. Trini Alvedo would tell him all he wanted to know. Penny. Her death gnawed at him.

Why hadn't she listened to him? The bold little TV anchorwoman wanted to get the best pictures possible for her story, of course. It would be a helluva story, too. Mark would see to it her television station would get her film and a full explanation about her efforts and sacrifice. He owed her that much. First he had to wring Trini dry and turn him over to the authorities.

Then he'd make a trip south of the border to the newest and most dangerous Marxist state in the Western Hemisphere.

13

WINDOW-SHOPPING

"Welcome to Guatemala, Captain Chaney," declared a portly, dark-skinned officer dressed in green fatigues with a silver eagle on each collar. He also wore a pistol in a battered brown leather holster on his hip and a grin on his round, olive face.

"Gracias, coronel," the Penetrator replied. He raised his hand to salute. The colonel had greeted him before he could climb from the black-painted State Department helio-courier.

"¡Ajá! ¿Habla usted español?" the Guatemalan officer inquired, enthused at the prospect. *"Bueno.* I am *Coronel* Manuel Fernando Raphael Santos-Brüchner. However, introductions are all we can safely discuss until we can talk in my office. *¿Comprende?"*

"Sí, Coronel Santos," Mark Hardin agreed. "A wise man always takes care to speak where unwanted ears do not listen."

"And these days such ears are all too common," Santos sighed.

Mark followed the colonel to his jeep. The Penetrator carried a U.S. Army duffel bag in one hand and used the other to secure the green beret on his head while he walked through the prop blast of the helio-courier. He felt odd, once again wearing an army uniform. This time with the "Sword and Lightning" shoulder patch of Special Forces on his sleeve. The black captain's bars on his fatigue-jacket collar and name tag—CHA-

NEY—on the left breast were the only other items he hadn't worn in Vietnam.

The Safari Arms MatchMaster in a GI shoulder holster strapped to his chest was another new addition. One of the most dependable, best-made, and most accurate .45 combat pistols ever made, the MatchMaster was roughly the same size and weight as a government issue 1911-A1. The Penetrator had never used a Safari Arms weapon on a mission before, but he'd been highly pleased by its performance on the firing range and he wanted his cover as an "adventuring Company man" to be complete. At the jeep, Mark and his duffel bag joined Colonel Santos in the back and the driver turned the key in the ignition.

They drove away from the isolated runway and rolled across the Guatemala City Airport—which also contained the country's main air force base. The northernmost of all Central American republics, Guatemala had a reputation as the "Land of Eternal Spring," and the pleasant climate proved that it was not without merit. The Penetrator also knew that Guatemala had the largest population in Central America and most of its 5 million people had ancestral roots in the ancient Mayans. Colonel Santos and his driver were evidence of this, since both men were clearly *mestizos.*

The jeep pulled up to a concrete building with a tin roof. Mark and Santos climbed out. The Penetrator suddenly noticed an old single-engine airplane on the field near a runway. It resembled the World War II fighters seen in *Twelve O'Clock High* or *Black Sheep Squadron,* though made several years later.

"You like antique aircraft, *capitán*?" Santos inquired with a bemused smile.

"I like just about any kind of aircraft if it is dependable, *coronel*," Mark replied. "The AT-Six-F was a fine fighter-bomber in its day. I haven't seen one in years. Does she fly?"

"She does indeed," Santos confirmed. "But didn't your country use them in Vietnam?"

"Yes, in a limited way. There were quite a few in-country, though not in my sector. They're beautiful birds."

Pride dictated the Guatemalan colonel's reply. "Our mechanics have babied that old plane and tuned it to a fine edge. She can still fight, too. It can handle modern rockets as well as less sophisticated weaponry. A useful trick we learned from you *norteamericanos* is napalm—which will allow us to give those Sandinistan trash a warm reception if they ever dare to cross our border, no?"

"Do you consider that to be a likely possibility?"

"If the Marxist scum aren't removed from Nicaragua and something done about Castro, it is a distinct possibility. But, that is why your government sent you," the colonel remarked. "Let us discuss this inside with a *cerveza* or two."

Although the colonel's office hardly needed air-conditioning, due to the mild climate, Santos turned on a wall unit and closed a window. Mark wasn't impressed by the officer's idea of security, but he kept his opinion to himself while Santos opened a small refrigerator and extracted two bottles of beer.

"We were surprised and quite pleased when we received the coded message to expect you, *Capitán* Chaney," Santos stated. "Of course, we realize Langley has taken an interest in the Sandinistans' activity in El Salvador for some time. We're glad your Central Intelligence Agency recognizes the threat to our country as well."

"A danger recognized is one half neutralized, *coronel*," Mark replied as he accepted a bottle. *"Gracias."*

The Penetrator wondered what Colonel Santos would say if he knew the radio message had no connection with the CIA. Since he'd relayed vital information about

Operation Plague Five to Dan Griggs, Mark had asked the Justice Department agent to return the favor. The Penetrator needed a solid cover before he headed to Central America, preferably one that would allow him to transport weapons and move into action as rapidly as possible. Thus, he became "Captain Richard Chaney" of U.S. Army Special Forces, assigned to a top-secret covert operation via the CIA.

Griggs and Professor Haskins had pulled enough strings to convince the Guatemalan government, and now it was up to Mark to play out the role and use it to complete his mission. Once again, as usual, the Penetrator was on his own.

"We have known of the dangers presented by Daniel Ortega's regime ever since his damned *comunistas* overthrew *Presidente* Somoza," Santos declared solemnly. "It is no secret—at least it isn't *now*—that Cuban and Soviet advisors are behind the present government in Nicaragua. Russian-style training centers are located throughout the country. Military installations have cropped up like maggots from rotting meat. The Sandinistan army now numbers over seventy thousand men.

"No other Central American country has an army close to that in manpower. Guatemala's military is larger than most of our neighbors, and we have less than fifteen thousand troops. Construction of new military airfields is almost completed between Puerto Cabezas and Julgalpa. The Russians then plan to deliver sixteen MIG fighter jets to Ortega. Nicaraguan pilots will soon complete training in Bulgaria. The Sandinistans will then have not only the largest army in Central America, but the most deadly air force as well."

"There is indeed cause for alarm, *coronel*," the Penetrator agreed. "For my country likewise. Recent intelligence acquired from U-2 overflights indicates considerable activity deep within the jungle regions of Nicaragua. The tropical rain forest provides an effective shield, even to the eyes of our best spy cameras; yet the photographs have been examined by physicists of the Nuclear Regulatory Commission and they suspect that a Soviet-style breeder reactor is being constructed in that area."

"A breeder reactor?" Santos's eyes bulged with alarm. "Is that not the type of nuclear facility that builds or breeds nuclear fuel for bombs and missiles?"

"Sí, coronel," Mark replied grimly. "I trust you understand why this matter must be dealt with by the most confidential means—and the utmost speed."

"¡Madre de Dios!" the colonel vehemently whispered. "What should we do? Launch an attack? Bomb the reactor like the Israelis did to Iraq before the *comunistas* can use it against us?"

"If there is no other way," the Penetrator confirmed. "Yet, we must consider two facts. First, the Sandinistans have Soviet antiaircraft guns located in the northwest, at Villa Nueva and near Lake Nicaragua at Diriamba. Second, we can not be certain that a breeder reactor is indeed being constructed until we have gone in and seen it for ourselves."

"And that is what you intend to do, *capitán*?" Santos couldn't have been more surprised if his guest had asked for a fully loaded revolver to play Russian roulette.

"That is what *must* be done—and soon," Mark stated. "The longer we wait, the more critical the situation becomes. If at all possible, I want to be in Nicaragua tonight."

Colonel Santos took a long gulp of beer, stared thoughtfully at the bottle, and then consumed the rest of its contents. "How many men will you need?"

"A small team of the *right* men. No more than four.

Preferably men who know the country, especially the jungles."

"I have such men under my command. As you know, many members of the Somoza *guardia nacional* fled the country after the junta took over. Most of them are in Honduras, but some came to my country. We also have a few Sandinistan defectors who became disillusioned with their revolution."

"You know your men, *coronel*," the Penetrator said. "I'll leave the selection of the team to you."

Santos nodded grimly. "Is Langley certain the situation is this critical, *capitán*?"

"Believe me," the Penetrator replied. "It is extremely critical."

By two o'clock in the afternoon, "Captain Chaney's" team had been assembled. Naturally, a Guatemalan had been made second in command. *Capitán* José Moreno proved to be a handsome young Latino who resembled a youthful Ricardo Montalban. Moreno had attended a military academy in Mexico City and trained with the U.S. Marines in the Canal Zone before the Torrijos regime was paid by the peanut pusher to take it over.

Lieutenant Amado Escutia and Sergeant Luis Mudeja were both former members of the Somoza *guardia nacional*. Otherwise, the two had little in common. Tall and lean, Escutia was forty-one years old, soft-spoken, and quick to smile, although Mark noticed his eyes seldom agreed with the upward curl of his lips. It was the smile of a man who had learned to accept disappointment.

Mark had immediate doubts about Mudeja, vague and uncertain though they were. If he, alone, had the choice of the team, he felt he would leave Mudeja behind. Colonel Santos had personally selected the team, and the Penetrator felt it wise not to countermand his host's decisions. Mudeja didn't seem to know how to smile. The bullish, fiery-eyed Nicaraguan regarded the others with surly suspicion. All except Corporal Urbaldo Sojeda. Mudeja's eyes dripped venom when he glanced at the last member of the team.

Sojeda appeared to be an undernourished *peón* dressed in an oversized military uniform. He had indeed been born in a poor village a few hundred kilometers from Granada in Nicaragua. He'd also been recruited into the Sandinistan rebel forces that overthrew Somoza. Unless his haggard features and sad eyes were a clever mask, Sojeda regretted his involvement with the Sandinistans.

After telling the men his fabricated story about the nuclear reactor, the Penetrator moved to a map sprawled across Colonel Santos's desk while he explained the plan to infiltrate Nicaragua.

"We'll leave tonight in a small fishing boat," Mark told them. "Of course, we'll be disguised as Nicaraguan fishermen. Civilians, poor social level, but legitimate employment. This means we'll carry a minimum of weapons and equipment. Once we get in, we can't call for help. Even if we do, no one will hear us. Understand?"

"*Sí,*" Moreno agreed. "And I assume we drift far enough into international waters of the Pacific to avoid detection of our origin before we head for the coast of Nicaragua?"

"Correct," Mark confirmed. "You *caballeros* know the country," he addressed the ex-Nicaraguans. "What do you think of the plan?"

"I think it is sound," Escutia stated. "But if we dock along the northwest coast, don't forget there is a large military installation at El Regate. We'd do well to avoid that, no?"

"We won't be able to avoid the damned Sandinistans," Mudeja hissed. "Those *comunista* lice are everywhere."

"We'll have to try," the Penetrator declared. "Don't forget, we're on a reconnaissance mission, sergeant," he softened the reprimand with a quick smile, then turned to Sojeda. "How well do you know the jungles, corporal?"

"I was raised in them," Sojeda answered quickly. "I know the rain forests of Nicaragua like a priest knows his church. When I was . . ." he hesitated, looking sheepishly at the floor. "Was a guerrilla, I was camped all over the jungles. We—I had to know them well."

Mudeja glared at Sojeda and started to speak. Mark lightly laid his hand on the sergeant's shoulder to get his attention. "We are all on the same side now, *amigo*. Remember that."

"*Capitán* Chaney?" Escutia began. "May I suggest that you allow us to handle most communications with native Nicaraguans when we arrive? Your Spanish is excellent, but it is not the Spanish of Central America. You could easily pass for a *mejicano,* but not as one of my countrymen."

"I agree, lieutenant," Mark told him. "Just don't forget that I'm in command. I'm certain Colonel Santos made that clear to you already. If any of you have questions or second thoughts about this mission, now is the time to voice them. After we leave this room, it'll be too late for any of us to back out."

The four men remained silent.

"*Bueno,*" the Penetrator declared. "Then let us prepare for our boat trip."

14

A VIEW OF TYRANNY

The capital city of Managua had been turned into an armed fortress. Soviet T-54 tanks and armored personnel carriers lumbered through the streets. Sandinistan troops, dressed in fatigue uniforms and armed with M-16 assault rifles that had been supplied to Nicaragua during the Somoza regime by the U.S. government, were everywhere. Cuban military advisors, clad in brown fatigues with a red star tacked to their caps, usually strolled along the sidewalks.

Hundreds of civilians shuffled through the streets of Managua. Most wore simple attire—short-sleeve shirts, slacks, loose-fitting dresses. Farmers and ranch laborers were clad in the straw sombreros, sandals, and white "pajama" shirt and trousers that symbolize poverty south of the U.S. border. All the civilians, regardless of their social status, avoided contact with the military. Uniforms represented the government and, in Nicaragua, authority meant brute force. The citizens had already learned to endure the excessive manipulations and restrictions characteristic of a Marxist state, without inviting its wrath.

Consequently, no one paid much attention to the five *peónes* who rolled a small wooden cart into an alley. Their puny wagon—which resembled a Chinese rickshaw in the same manner the *peónes* seemed not unlike coolies—was loaded with dead fish and there seemed nothing suspicious about seeking shade for such a cargo when the noon sun dominated the sky. Perhaps an astute observer noticed that one of the five men towered above his companions. Few natives of Nicaragua stand over six feet tall. Yet this was merely an oddity and not a cause for alarm, so the fishermen were ignored by soldier and civilian alike.

This attitude suited the desires of the Penetrator and his four teammates. Mark Hardin watched a Russian tank rumble across the crudely paved street like a mechanical elephant, followed by a batallion of wooden-faced Sandinistans on the march. *We've reached Managua,* he thought. Not a bad start.

Indeed, the recon mission into Nicaragua had thus far been blessed with good fortune. Mark and his four men had drifted to the northwest coast near El Regate. If their arrival had been observed by the military, no one considered the fishing boat worth investigating. Thankful for the darkness and with little exchange of words, they wrapped most of their weapons and other gear in oilcloth and placed the bundles in the cart before covering them with mounds of fish.

The team then located a dirt road. With the aid of a compass and the memories of the three Nicaraguan-born team members, they headed southwest. By dawn they approached Lake Managua, taking care to avoid Jiloa, where a Soviet-style Special Forces training center had been constructed. From there, they moved on to the capital city.

"What do we do now, *capitán*?" Mudeja demanded in a harsh whisper.

"Don't address me by rank," the Penetrator told him. "Call me Ricardo. As for our next move, we keep our ears and eyes open and our mouths shut, unless we have a damn good reason to speak—and we try to find a lead to the reactor's location."

"Play it on the ear," Escutia remarked with a grin. "Like you *norteamericanos* say."

Mark nodded. Escutia had the right idea even if he didn't have the metaphor down pat. "After we get our fish to the marketplace, we'll split up. Luis will stay with the cart, Amado will go with José, and I'll take Urbaldo."

"But how are we supposed to learn anything about this atomic installation that way?" Mudeja demanded, rolling a cigarette with ease. "I say we grab one of the Sandinistan bigshots or, better yet, one of Castro's *bastardos,* and make him tell us. Give me an hour with the scum. I'll make him talk."

The Penetrator smiled tolerantly. "You'd make him yell all right, but taking someone like that is more apt to attract the soldiers and the secret police than solve our problem."

Mudeja glared at Mark. "You *gringos* always want to talk and talk or try to solve all your difficulties with money. You have no courage. That is why your country lost its claim to the Panama Canal and why you turned your face from *Presidente* Somoza and allowed the *communistas* to seize control. You are no better than the Russians . . ."

Shit, the Penetrator thought. He knew he was going to have trouble with this surly hot-head. He should have kicked him off the team before they left Guatemala, Colonel Santos or not. Mark glanced around to be certain none of the soldiers or civilians were watching.

Satisfied they were unobserved, the Penetrator suddenly sprang onto Mudeja like a jaguar. Both men toppled into the filth of the alley, Mark on top of the sergeant. While the other three team members watched in astonishment, he rammed Mudeja's head against the ground twice and then pinned the Nicaraguan's arms under his knees.

The Penetrator's hand streaked to the back of his neck and found the Micarta slab handles of the Bowie-

Axe he wore in a special harness sheath between his shoulder blades. Luis Mudeja's eyes swelled when he saw the heavy-bladed knife start to descend.

Mark brought the Bowie-Axe down in a fast, chopping stroke, then stopped the motion a quarter of an inch from Mudeja's throat. The sergeant gasped when he felt the thick steel under his chin and the razor-sharp edge against his flesh.

"You question my courage, Luis?" Mark hissed vehemently. "You insult my country and compare us to the *soviéticos.* I'll cut your head off unless you apologize and give me your word that you will not use your tongue in such an offensive manner again."

Mudeja's mouth moved silently. The Penetrator felt his stomach knot. He regretted such a theatrical display, particularly one involving a leading NCO, and a good one at that. But he knew that if he was to maintain command of the mission he couldn't allow the others to doubt his *maschismo.* If Mudeja didn't respond to his demands immediately, Mark would have to kill him.

"I, ah, spoke in haste, *capitán,*" Mudeja rasped. "It angers me to see the Sandinistans ruling my homeland. I did not mean the things I said . . ."

"Do I have your word?" the Penetrator whispered an inch from his face.

"Sí, capitán." Mudeja replied quickly.

"Capitán? Can't you follow any order, Luis?"

"¿Qué?" the sergeant blinked. "Oh, *¡Sí, Ricardo!"*

"That's better," Mark declared. He smiled and slid the Bowie back into its sheath, then rose. Mudeja slowly got to his feet. "I can understand that what you see here upsets you, Luis," the Penetrator assured him, hoping to sooth the man's dignity. "A calm mind is better than a short temper. You can enjoy the kill more with a clear head—and you can relish its memory forever in perfect recall. *¿Comprende?"*

Mudeja smiled for the first time.

"But the time has not yet come to kill, and we should not make enemies with each other while surrounded by thousands of opponents," Mark added. "Now, let's move on to the marketplace and try to find the location of our main target. The sooner we do this, the faster the time for killing will arrive."

Captain Moreno, Lieutenant Escutia, and Corporal Sojeda stared at their commander, stunned by this cobra speed and cold-blooded philosophy. Mudeja grinned with delight. He'd found a soldier after his own heart. They rolled the fish cart out of the alley and moved on.

The marketplace of Managua proved to be slightly less somber than the rest of the city. Although propaganda posters plastered the walls and soldiers patrolled the area, their attitude seemed more casual. Civilian merchants, farmers, weavers, and fishermen stood by carts and crudely made stands, trying to sell their merchandise to anyone with a few *centavos* to spare. Business wasn't good. Most Nicaraguans didn't appear to be interested in purchasing the goods and the peddlers' wares weren't plentiful. Only the hat makers and cigar makers seemed well stocked.

Ah, the joys of Marxism, the Penetrator mused.

The Utopian theories of socialism were unrealistic at best and generally devastating in actual practice. The Gospel According to Saint Marx taught that all the world's ills stemmed from some having more than others, and the economics of Communism proported to divide everything equally among everyone. Thus everything belonged to the state: goods, services, and even people's lives. Naturally, the rulers took their share in advance. Nicaragua had an enormous military for a country its size, and it owed its soul to the company store—in Moscow. The state's cut was huge, and what little remained for the average Nicaraguan citizen proved to be precious small indeed. So much for Utopia.

After they found enough space to park the fish cart, Luis Mudeja remained with the wagon, gossiping with other merchants, while Mark and the others mingled with the crowd. All five men appreciated the risks involved in the mission.

Both Latin American countries and Communist governments traditionally plant informers and undercover agents among the populace. *Anyone* could be a spy for Ortega, Havana, or the Kremlin, or for all of the above. One suspicious act or word could ruin their plan.

If the authorities tried to search any of the team members or their cart, they'd either face capture or have to fight. Both actions meant certain death, but a choice between vivisection by the secret police or dying swiftly in a gun battle was no choice at all.

While Captain Moreno and Lieutenant Escutia wandered toward a row of stands and carts, Mark and Corporal Sojeda headed for the nearest *cantina*. Whether it be a cocktail lounge in Beverly Hills, a pool hall in Harlem, a British pub, or a German *bierstube*, the tavern remained one of the most reliable sources for current gossip and local rumors. Alcohol loosens tongues and the relaxed atmosphere of a saloon tends to make one talkative. However, Mark realized this fact would surely be common knowledge to the authorities, and the ears of Ortega's junta—and possibly the KGB—might lurk inside the *cantinas*.

Two hours later, the Penetrator and Sojeda entered the third tavern they had selected to visit. Four big wooden spools that had once held copper cables served as tables, and customers sat on empty crates with Cyrillic Russian printed on the boxes. A weary bartender leaned on a flat-topped counter and nodded while two patrons exchanged tales of personal woe. A film of dust had settled on the floor and a blue-gray fog of smoke rose from cigarettes and pipes. Mark and Sojeda approached the bar.

"Dos cervezas, por favor," Sojeda ordered.

"The beer is warm, *amigos*," the bartender warned them. "The *americano* refrigeration has broken down again. The tequila is good. The *koro* worms give it a fine flavor."

"Cerveza will be fine," Sojeda assured him.

The bartender sighed and rinsed out two glass mugs in a pan of greasy water. Mark glanced at the two old men who sat at a spool-table. Their eyes seemed empty. They simply drank tequila, licked salt, and smoked their pipes without conversation.

"Yesterday," one of the young Nicaraguans at the bar began, "I went to old Diego to see about doing some work on his plantation."

"What do you know about coffee?" the other customer scoffed. "You do not even drink it." He poked a finger into his friend's paunchy belly.

"¡Mierda!" the first man exclaimed. "You know better than that. I may not know anything about growing coffee shrubs and I'm not yet desperate enough to pick those damn beans all day for a few *quetzals,* but I am good with my hands. I am a carpenter and Diego's house often needs repairs or a bit of painting here and there."

"Dos cervezas," the bartender observed in a bored manner while he placed two tall, thin glasses of beer on the counter in front of Mark and Sojeda. The Penetrator paid him sixty *centavos* and raised his *tubo* to his lips. The beer was flat and warm.

"Well, Diego was not there," the customer continued his story. "Instead, I found the Sandinistans had taken over the plantation. They told me Diego was an enemy of the state, a capitalist who had conspired with Somoza, and they had liberated his *peónes* from oppression. Liberated? *¡Hijo de la chingada!* I saw them still working on the hills, picking coffee beans like before, only now they have soldiers watching them and they receive but half of what Diego paid them. Son of a bitch!" he repeated himself, "if that is 'liberated,' I don't want any of it."

"What happened to Diego?" his companion inquired.

"I did not ask. Would you have done so?"

"Do I look so stupid?" Both customers and the bartender shook their heads.

"Then an officer, a *cubano* in a brown uniform, he asks why I am there. I told him I am a carpenter and I did a little work for Diego from time to time. He looks at me like I just told him I'd raped his youngest daughter. 'You mean you make more income than your job allows?' the pig demands. 'Does the government know about this? You can not make a profit unless it is approved by the Ministry of Labor,' he says. 'And then, that decision must be approved.' 'By whom, *señor*?' I ask him. 'We must approve all decisions,' he tells me. *We* approve it, this *cubano* scum says as though this is *his* country! Then he tells me that I should not be greedy and I should accept my equal share as the others do. My share? What the government gives me hardly feeds my children and lets me keep my store open. If this *cubano* believes in equality, why does he wear an officer's rank? He ought to be out there picking coffee beans like a *peón*."

"It is not wise to speak of such things," the bartender advised, nodding toward the Penetrator and Sojeda, whom he'd never seen before, and pouring more tequila into the man's glass. "Here, this is on the house."

"*¡Bastardos!*" the carpenter hissed.

"*Ay,* Roberto!" his companion chided, but he glanced nervously at Mark and Sojeda. "Things are not so bad. I remember how you once spoke of Somoza. At least we no longer have to tolerate that *cabrón, ¿verdad?*"

"Somoza ruled with a steel fist and he put heavy taxes on us and his family controlled most of the industries and big plantations," Roberto confirmed. "And what they didn't own, they soon did. But he didn't treat a man like a criminal because he tried to earn a few *quetzals*."

"He was too friendly with the damned *gringos*," the other man declared.

"And what of Ortega and his alliance with the Cubans and the Russians?" Roberto growled. "At least the *norteamericanos* didn't come to Nicaragua with tanks and planes and tell us, 'this is *my* country'! Somoza didn't turn our land into a giant military fortress and talk about going to war with our neighbors. I tell you—"

Roberto's sentence abruptly ended when two men dressed in green fatigue uniforms entered the *cantina*. The Sandinistan troopers strolled arrogantly to the bar. Roberto and his friend quickly made room for the soldiers. Mark and Sojeda moved to the far end of the counter.

"Tequila, comrade," one of the Sandinistans ordered. "Charge it to the state!" He and his companion laughed.

Roberto and his friend decided to leave. The old men at the spool-table barely looked up, apparently undisturbed by the soldiers. They had seen too much injustice, too much oppression. They would enjoy what peace they could find with strong drink and silence.

The Sandinistans unslung their M-16 rifles and propped the pieces against the counter. One of the men sighed and shook his head. "This duty in Managua is tiresome. The only thing worse than monotony is taking orders from *soviético* technicians at Diriambe.

I had to do that for almost a year, so I guess I shouldn't complain too much."

"You should have been stationed in Matagalpa," the other soldier responded. He rolled his eyes toward the ceiling. "Go too far into the jungle and your own comrades would shoot you."

"What do you mean, Guillermo?" the first trooper inquired. He grabbed a bottle from the bartender before the man could pour a drink. "*Gracias,* I'll take this one. Now, get one for *mi amigo,* too."

"*Sí,*" the bartender replied with a shrug.

"You two!" Guillermo suddenly accosted Mark and Sojeda. "You stink of dead fish. Bring a good catch into the market today, eh, fishermen?"

"*Sí,* Camarada," Sojeda answered with a weak smile. "We were fortunate. It has been a long day and it is hot, so we thought some *cerveza* would be welcome in dry throats—"

"Do not lie to me, *chico,*" Guillermo interrupted, glaring at the pair. Sojeda swallowed nervously. The Penetrator's hand slipped under his loose-fitting shirt and eased toward the grips of the Safari MatchMaster in his waistband. "You *peónes* don't *think*! You just mill about dully from one day to the next like an *estúpida vaca,* no?"

"If you say so, *camarada,*" Sojeda agreed meekly.

Guillermo laughed. Then he fixed his eyes on Mark. "Your *amigo* is a man of few words. What's wrong? Are you too dumb to understand me?"

"*Sí,*" the Penetrator answered with a shrug. "I am just an *estúpido* like all the other cows. Mooo!"

Guillermo and his companion laughed, failing to notice anything odd about Mark's accent. "You are a big cow, fisherman. Maybe you should join the army and we can cut off your udders and give you some balls, no? Miguel D'Escoto is now our foreign minister.

If they can put *huevos* on a priest, they can put them on anything."

"Forget about these two," the other soldier urged. "Tell me about this business in the jungle near Matagalpa."

"Maybe I shouldn't," Guillermo replied. "No one is supposed to know about it. Especially the *soviéticos* and the *cubanos.*"

"Cristo! We grew up in the same village. I hate the Russian pigs, and the *cubanos* are nothing but Russians who speak better Spanish. This is Ernesto you're talking to, Memo."

Guillermo sighed. "Don't tell anyone what I say, agreed?" He obviously didn't consider anyone else present to be in a position to threaten his secret.

"Agreed," Ernesto muttered in disgust. "So what happened?"

"When I was stationed at Matagalpa," Guillermo began, glancing at the doorway in case anyone wearing a uniform stood there, "my company was sent into the jungle to clear a path so the Russians will have some place to drive their tanks and armored cars. We were told not to go too far to the northeast. While we were working on the road, someone hears this noise. It was a loud, high-pitched whine. Then this cloud appears from nowhere. It looked like a tornado at first, but it was smaller and green."

Ernesto chuckled. Guillermo loved to spin tall tales and this one sounded like one of his best. "What had you been drinking that day, Memo?"

"It is true," Guillermo insisted. "This funnel cloud was a swarm of locusts. I've never seen insects fly in such a tight pattern before, but they swooped overhead and moved straight for the whine as though it called to them."

The Penetrator fought to control his expression. He

kept his eyes from turning toward the soldiers. No need to look at them. Just listen. Ernesto shook his head.

"Ridículo," he muttered.

"*Mierda.* I know what I saw," Guillermo insisted. "If you don't believe me, go fuck yourself!"

"All right," his friend sighed. "What happened then?" Ernesto was beginning to enjoy himself, this was one hell of a tale.

"We went into the jungle to get a better look. We were about eighty kilometers from Matagalpa on that damn road. Sweat and mosquitoes and hard rock to blast every centimeter of the way. Well, we never finished it. After what happened, they ordered that the road be built somewhere else."

"You'll never finish the story either at this rate," Ernesto grunted.

"We entered the jungle and followed the locust. There must have been a million of those insects. Anyway, we marched through that green hell and what do we see? Buildings, Ernesto. There were huge buildings that looked like greenhouses and the tornado of locusts were pouring right into the center of it."

Ernesto cast a dubious eye. "Is this another of your jokes, Memo?"

Guillermo glared at him. "I swear by the soul of my mother," he began. "There was also a tall building, made of steel and glass, like a *gringo* skyscraper, but shorter. In front of it stood several men. Some dressed in white coats, like doctors, others in strange uniforms. Not all of them were Latinos and I don't think any were Russians. A tall, slim Oriental seemed to be in charge. His face was sharp, with cruel, slanted eyes, and he smiled with the satisfied expression of *el lobo* when it finds a wounded calf."

"You got that close?" Ernesto incredulously inquired.

"No, *estúpido.* I used binoculars."

"What has this to do with someone taking a shot at you, *amigo*?"

Guillermo nodded hard. "They did! Several soldiers *dressed in our uniforms* suddenly appeared and opened fire on us. Two of my comrades were killed. The rest of us fled. When we reported the incident to our *capitán*, he sent us to *coronel* Montoya. The colonel told us that we had seen nothing, that it was top secret, and we were not to mention it to anyone. The next day we were ordered to pack our gear and they sent us from Matagalpa. Most of us were glad to leave after that."

"What do you think they were doing there?" Ernesto mused.

"I don't know and I don't want to know and I wish I hadn't opened my mouth about it," Guillermo burst out. "Let's take our bottles and try to find some women. This *cantina* is more boring than an empty stable."

Mark Hardin raised his beer and drank, not tasting the flat, warm brew. A secret complex that controlled the actions of insects with an Oriental commander in charge. The Penetrator had found the location of the headquarters of the Plague Five conspiracy and his old nemesis Colonel Po.

15

DEATH MARKET

The jeep bounced harshly along the crude dirt path that could only be called a road if one had a vivid imagination and a generous attitude toward terminology. The Penetrator tilted the green cap back from his eyes while he drove. The hat fit poorly, but the fatigue shirt was a joke.

Its former owner had been a short, fat Sandinistan, yet his clothing best suited Mark's broad chest. The sleeves were rolled up to his elbows and he still wore white cotton trousers, although fortunately he'd had a pair of paratrooper boots among the gear hidden in the fish cart.

His four team members had been lucky enough to acquire uniforms that fit their smaller frames. Ambushing a few Sandinistans hadn't been difficult. The soldiers hadn't expected trouble from a handful of *peónes* and the fallen tree in the road seemed a natural obstacle. When the patrol stopped, Mark and Captain Moreno simply pulled their pistols and told the men to get out of the jeep. They ordered the soldiers to strip and then Sergeant Mudeja cut the Marxist minions' throats. The team repeated the procedure with another vehicle and obtained five uniforms and extra gasoline.

"I still don't understand why we bothered with the uniforms," Lieutenant Escutia remarked. "If what you

146

heard in the *cantina* is correct, the guards in the jungle will open fire on us anyway."

Captain Moreno groaned with annoyance. Second lieutenants were the same everywhere. "First we have to get to the jungle, no? This way the soldiers will not be apt to stop us. Five *peónes* in a jeep would certainly attract attention. Use your head, Amado."

"My head tells me it must look suspicious for anyone to be driving on a road that everyone knows wasn't completed," Escutia responded dryly. "But then, who is going to see us?"

"Maybe the men in the jungle," Sojeda added grimly. "They might open fire on us at any moment." He gripped the frame of a confiscated M-16 as he spoke, trying to find comfort in the weapon.

"They won't ambush us on the road," the Penetrator assured his team. "The hidden complex is supposed to be a secret and they won't do anything to attract attention."

"What bothers me is the claim that the installation is commanded by an Oriental," Moreno stated, checking his Obregon .45 automatic. "If this is the Soviet nuclear reactor your *norteamericano* intelligence discovered, why would an Oriental be in charge? Why would this *Coronel* Montoya warn his soldiers not to mention it to anyone—especially the Russians?"

"I know of this Montoya," Sojeda declared. "I remember him when we were still involved in the guerrilla wars with Somoza. Montoya was one of Daniel Ortega's most trusted aides. Often, he was involved in covert operations that even the Sandinistan generals and our Cuban allies were unaware of."

Mudeja spat angrily. "You've seen what your beloved comrades have done to our country, Sojeda. Do you like it? Are you proud of what you helped to accomplish?"

Before Mark could tell Mudeja to shut up, Sojeda

answered. "No, I am not proud that I was once one of them. And I do not approve of what has happened, but do you think I am responsible? I was a *peón* in a small village, illiterate and ignorant of politics. Do not forget that Somoza wanted us to be that because uneducated minds could not plot against him. Then the Sandinistas came. They told us they needed recruits for their rebel forces and they took me and other young men. Our families were transported to a 'camp' for their 'protection.' We knew what that meant. We could either fight with the rebels or our families would suffer. If I believed in those *communistas* I would still be one of them, no? Perhaps I am not free of blame, but how much can you place on my shoulders, *sargento*?"

"I did two tours in Vietnam," the Penetrator added. "Once in a while I got a chance to talk to a Vietcong or an NVA soldier who had defected from the Reds. Some of them worked with the American military, especially the marine corps. They were nicknamed Kit Carson Scouts. The defectors told me that the Cong or the NVA would march into villages and recruit men the same way. Urbaldo was a victim of the Sandinistas and now he's one of us, so get off his back, Luis."

"*Capitán* Chaney," Moreno said in a weary voice. "I repeat my question: How do we know the complex mentioned by those soldiers is the nuclear reactor?"

"We don't," Mark admitted, feeling the strain of maintaining the fiction. "But everything seems to suggest it is. The high-pitched whine might well be the turbogenerators powered by the reactor. The acoustics of such a sound often attract certain insect species, especially if the digithermalator is operating at its peak." He hoped none of the others realized he didn't know what the hell he was talking about. "As for the Oriental, it is entirely possible Ortega has formed an alliance with another foreign power and neglected to mention this to the Russians or the Cubans."

"You mean the *chinos*?" Escutia inquired with amazement.

"Why not?" Mark shrugged. "The Chinese have competed with the Soviets before, in Southeast Asia, Africa, the Middle East. More than one sharp ruler has seen the value of playing both sides against each other."

"But how could they build a nuclear complex right under the noses of the Russians?" Moreno persisted.

"Who says they did?" the Penetrator answered. "The Chinese are old hands at the espionage business. They wrote the book on the subject—literally. The *Ping Fa* by Sun Tzu in the year 510 B.C. could be called the first masterpiece on organizing a spy network. And don't underestimate Chinese technology. They're a highly inventive people and they're good at keeping secrets."

"Sí," Escutia nodded. "And if the goal is worthwhile, the *chinos* can be most patient."

"That's a luxury we can't afford," Mark observed.

They reached the end of the incomplete road. Dense vegetation formed a formidable horseshoe around them. Trees with oversized leaves, waist-high grass, and cords of tangled vines seemed to present an impenetrable wall everywhere. Mark turned to Sojeda.

"You're the expert on the jungles around here," he said. "What's your advice?"

"We go to the northeast," Sojeda answered, drawing a machete from its scabbard. "The soldiers have been warned not to wander off in that direction and there are mountains in that region. There the complex would have access to fresh water without being close to the well-populated areas around Lake Nigaragua and Managua. Plenty food, too: bananas, papayas, sapodilla trees with plum fruit, and monkeys and small deer for meat to supplement dry rations."

The five men attacked the foliage with jungle knives. Tall grass and shrubbery fell beneath the slashing blades. They ducked under low branches and tried to avoid tangles of vines and tree roots. The humid conditions contributed to the eighty-degree temperature and their constant labor soon bathed them in their own sweat.

Of the team members, ironically, Lieutenant Escutia and Sergeant Mudeja had the most trouble coping with the tropical rain forest. Although Nicaraguan by birth, both men had been products of the cities. The Penetrator handled the environment well. He'd had more than his share of jungle combat missions in Vietnam, Panama, Angola, and Brazil. Captain Moreno's special training helped him bear up under the task, and Urbaldo Sojeda had no difficulty at all. He'd been bred to a life in a tropical rain forest. The jungles of Nicaragua were his home.

In the distance, the purple peaks of mountains taunted them—an elusive goal that seemed no closer after hours of fighting the vegetation. They continued to hack and struggle through the undergrowth. Escutia gasped and recoiled when one of the "vines" suddenly raised its head and flicked a pink, forked tongue at him. The others recognized the snake, a rosy boa, and assured Escutia it was harmless. Sojeda, however, noticed an innocent-looking tree with red applelike fruit and warned his companions not to touch it.

"La manzachila," he explained. "The fruit, bark, even the leaves are poisonous."

Mark stiffened when he saw a cluster of large, dark ants feasting on the corpse of a lizard as big as a house cat. The insects didn't advance toward the team and the Penetrator sighed with relief. Not all bugs were affected by the pheromonal magic of the Plague Five laboratories—at least, *not yet*.

Finally, the mountains grew closer and the forest became less formidable. The men put their machetes away and dealt with the foliage as best they could, bare-handed. Stealth became imperative. Twilight had fallen and the darkness assisted their efforts. Then they saw the enemy camp situated in a clearing at the base of a mountain.

"Madre de Dios," Escutia whispered in disbelief.

A column of enormous buildings, similar to a row of giant greenhouses, covered an area almost a mile in diameter. Sandinistan troops patrolled the complex, wearily marching back and forth. A two-story wooden structure, probably a barracks, stood to the west of the greenhouses. Positioned at the foot of the mountain in the center of the installation, a four-story structure of concrete, steel, and glass seemed to dominate the encampment.

"I do not think this is a nuclear power plant of any kind," Captain Moreno whispered softly.

"But I think we'd better find out exactly what the hell it *is*," the Penetrator rasped.

Hernando Becerric listened to the familiar serenade of the chattering monkeys, shrill-voiced birds, and various insects that made nightly performances in the jungle. He glanced at the surrounding vegetation and grunted sourly. "We fight to liberate Nicaragua," the leaders of the movement had claimed during the long, bloody guerrilla wars with the Somoza *guardia nacional*. Nicaragua had been "liberated," and where did that leave Becerric? Still stuck in a stinking jungle. What *loco* scheme did Ortega have in mind? He talked about preparing for war with Honduras, Guatemala, Costa Rica, and even the United States of America!

The junta had formed a partnership with the Soviets and the Cubans and a covert alliance with the Chinese and their Third World allies as well. If the Russians found out about that, what would happen? Managua would be blown to hell and Colonel Po's installation would be reduced to a pile of hot ashes and twisted metal—and there wouldn't be enough of Hernando Becerric left to be a cinder in someone's eye.

He noticed the shape of another sentry patroling the opposite end of the camp's perimeter. *Estúpido,* Becerric thought. No attack force would try to penetrate the jungle. One day, a Soviet spy plane would locate the installation and the Russians would shoot a missile down their throats. Becerric removed a tobacco pouch and a pack of rolling papers and began to make a cigarette. Such folly, he mused. We're all as good as dead.

Such thoughts proved most appropriate. A strong hand suddenly snaked from behind Becerric and clamped its palm over the Sandinistan's mouth. Becerric barely had time to realize he was about to die before he felt the terrible, hot pain of a bayonette in his right kidney.

The other guard turned in time to see Luis Mudeja finish off Becerric with a vicious throat slice. He didn't see or hear Urbaldo Sojeda when the ex-guerrilla silently crept from the jungle behind him, a machete held firmly in both hands. He raised the jungle knife and swung. The heavy blade chopped through the back of the guard's skull and cleaved his medulla into bloody, gray mush.

A third sentry whirled when he heard a stifled groan. José Moreno sprang from the tree line and swiftly draped a wire garrote over the man's head. A savage twist tightened the steel noose around the guard's throat and a knee to the kidney did the rest. The

Sandinistan's throat was cut open, his windpipe crushed, and his neck broken in a matter of seconds.

The fourth sentry heard the scuffle of feet and bolted from the edge of the perimeter to investigate. The Penetrator cursed under his breath. The others had acted before he could get into position to take out his target. Mark quickly stepped from the tree line and raised his Bowie-Axe, cocking it to his ear.

"*¡Aqui esta, camarada!*" he called softly.

Startled, the sentry turned. The Penetrator hurled his knife.

The Bowie-Axe turned once in midair, the razor edge glittering beneath the matte-black blade. It slammed into the guard's chest, point first. The sharp tip bit through flesh and muscle, cracked the third rib, and entered the man's heart. He collapsed in a twitching heap and died.

Mark adjusted the shoulder strap of his .45 caliber Ingram M-10 and approached his victim. He knelt by the dead soldier, pulled the Bowie-Axe from still-quivering flesh, and wiped the blade clean on the guard's shirt. Lieutenant Escutia emerged from the jungle behind Mark, a canvas pack strapped to his back and an M-16 held ready in his fists. The other members of the team drew closer until everyone could recognize each other and affirmitive nods assured them the only casualties belonged to the enemy.

The team moved into prearranged positions. Mudeja and Sojeda crouched by one of the greenhouses and trained their assault rifles on the barracks while Escutia and Moreno watched the headquarters building. The Penetrator turned his attention to the first greenhouse. He already knew what waited inside. It was a large breeding center for insects, far bigger than the structures he'd found at the New Mexico base.

The end of the Plague Five nightmare was finally in sight. The backpack carried by Escutia contained four pounds of C-4 plastic explosive, enough to destroy most, if not all, of Colonel Po's complex. Mark also wanted to get to the records inside the headquarters. He'd then be able to hunt out the remaining bases and destroy them. Though even if they had to lose the flies, after they cut off the brains of the operation, the threat of the smaller units would be relatively minimal.

The harsh metallic chatter of an automatic weapon suddenly ripped the night. Mark turned and saw two figures at the entrance of the HQ building. Orange flame spat from the muzzle of an M-16 in one man's hands. Another assault rifle replied and the two figures danced awkwardly as high-velocity bullets smashed into their bodies.

Shouts of alarm mingled with the cries of startled night birds and monkeys in the surrounding trees. Mark heard a tremendous angry hum within the greenhouse. The insects had been disturbed also. The building seemed to vibrate from the mere sound of the buzzing creatures. What were they? Bees? Wasps? There could be millions of the insects inside the structure.

Rifle-toting men appeared at the mouth of the barracks. Mudeja and Sojeda opened fire and M-16 rounds punched the soldiers' flesh. The troopers crumpled to the porch, dead before they could fire a shot.

The deep-throated rattle of a heavier caliber machine gun roared from the HQ building. *Shit,* Mark thought bitterly. Colonel Po had trained his men well and prepared his base to defend itself against an attack. The muzzle flare of a mounted machine gun lit up the compound and 7.62mm bullets burned the air.

The Penetrator crouched behind the greenhouse while a column of dust devils spat up from the ground from a volley of copper-jacketed projectiles. He didn't try to return fire. The Ingram's short-range capability made such an effort pointless. Something moved to

Mark's right. He pivoted on his knee and raised the M-10 before he recognized Captain José Moreno.

"What do we do now, Ricardo?" the Latino asked, desperation accenting his voice.

"We've got to try to take out that main building," the Penetrator answered solemnly. "No matter what the price. It has to be destroyed."

"We can't do it," Moreno replied helplessly. "Lieutenant Escutia is dead. The machine gun cut him to pieces. I couldn't reach him to retrieve the explosives. We're lucky the bullets didn't set them off."

"C-Four can't be detonated that way," Mark said sharply. "You know better than that. Don't get panic-stricken, José."

"But what will we do?" the Guatemalan officer insisted.

Mudeja and Sojeda dashed from their position and ran toward Mark and Moreno. Another mounted machine gun had been set up at the entrance of the barracks. The NCOs had been forced to flee a murderous cross fire of 7.62 steel.

Sojeda barely reached the cover of the greenhouse. Luis Mudeja wasn't that lucky. Machine-gun slugs tore into him like deadly hailstones. His body seemed to explode even as he ran. Torn pieces of cloth hopped from his uniform, accompanied by chunks of bloodied flesh. Mudeja screamed once and crashed heavily to the ground. Another volley of 7.62mm rounds kicked his corpse across the dust.

"Capitán," Sojeda said breathlessly. "We saw men moving behind the buildings. Soon, they will have us surrounded."

"Figures," Mark grimly allowed. "They don't want to put too many bullet holes in the greenhouses. If they can get to us with small arms or force us into the open, we've had it."

"You're in command, *amigo*," Moreno sighed. "I just hope you make the right decision."

The Penetrator's teeth ground together in anger. "We have to retreat," he admitted. "Or at least, let's give it a damn good try."

He removed three WP grenades from his ditty bag and gave two of them to Moreno and Sojeda. "When I count to three, you throw your grenade that way, José," he pointed toward the headquarters building. "Urbaldo, you throw at the barracks and I'll try to lob mine somewhere in between. Let's pray that the sudden glare and wall of fire will startle and disorient the enemy long enough for us to make our break."

Moreno and Sojeda nodded in mute reply.

"Uno—dos—tres!"

The trio of grenades hurled into the air and fell to earth. They exploded in unison, white phosphorous spilling across the ground like a pool of flaming gasoline. The glare blinded the unprepared forces of Colonel Po's personal army. They cried out in fear when the brilliant white bursts erupted. It seemed a supernova had suddenly taken place before their eyes.

Mark and his remaining teammates had already dashed from their position. They ran to the jungle and plunged into the vegetation. Desperately, they fought their way through the dense vines and tree limbs, aware that enemy bullets could pierce their backs at any moment. One emotion dominated the Penetrator's thought as he fled. It filled his mouth with a flavor of salt and copper fillings.

The bitter taste of defeat.

16

BATTLE SWARM

The Penetrator washed the bristles of hair from his razor and watched them flow down the drain. He wiped his freshly shaved face with rubbing alcohol and winced at the sting. He grinned weakly at the haggard face in the mirror. Actually, Mark had enjoyed a rare privilege. How many *gringos* get to shower and shave in the personal bathroom of a Guatemalan colonel?

Mark, Captain Moreno, and Corporal Sojeda had returned to Guatemala in a fishing boat five days after they departed the Plague Five site. Following their escape from the installation, they'd driven the jeep back toward Matagalpa. Aware that Po might contact Colonel Montoya or another Sandinistan officer involved in the operation, Mark stopped the vehicle after they'd put a few miles between themselves and Po's complex. Then he and his men removed their uniforms and once again donned fishermen apparel.

The Penetrator punched a hole in the gas tank and set fire to the jeep to destroy the uniforms and prevent Po's henchmen from realizing they had assumed a disguise. Regretfully, they had been forced to leave behind the Ingram and M-16s as well. Armed only with pistols and knives, they began the tedious, dangerous trek toward the border.

Eventually they reached Somoto, near the Nicaragua-Honduras border. Biding their time and hoping that

their luck would hold a while longer, the trio managed
to slip past the guards and barbed wire into Honduras,
where they were immediately apprehended by that
country's military. Fortunately, a training camp for Nicaraguan exiles was located nearby and their reception
proved to be cautiously friendly.

A radio message from *Coronel* Santos at the Guatemalan military base confirmed Mark's story about a
secret mission into Nicaragua. The Honduran authorities returned all personal belongings to the trio, including their weapons, and sent them on their way.

Colonel Santos wasn't there to meet them when
they reached Guatemala City. Captain Sanchez, the
colonel's aide, explained that Santos had gone to the
capital to a special meeting with *Presidente* Guevara.
The colonel proved to be a hospitable host even while
absent. He had left instructions that "Captain Chaney"
be allowed to use his personal quarters to rest and
recuperate after his ordeal—and to prepare a full report about what he had learned.

The Penetrator didn't have time to rest. His mission—
the real mission—had to be completed, and quickly.
Mark formulated a plan. It was desperate and highly
risky and he could see a hundred different ways it
could go wrong, probably getting himself killed in the
process. Yet, there wasn't any choice. Mark could
either take that last, slim chance or allow the Plague
Five operation to grow and eventually bring the entire
Western Hemisphere to its knees.

Dressed in a neatly pressed U.S. Army fatigue
uniform, polished paratrooper boots, and green Special Forces beret, Mark buckled on his GI shoulder
holster with the MatchMaster .45 cocked and locked
and strolled from the colonel's quarters. He walked to
the old AT-6-F bomber. A quick inspection assured
him Santos's claim that the old post–World War II

fighter plane was in prime working condition was true.
Next, he located a flight crew in a nearby hanger.

"You men," he snapped in his best, authoritative
voice. "*Coronel* Santos wants that plane fully armed
and ready to take off as soon as possible."

The five mechanics stared at the Penetrator in astonishment. "You mean that old *norteamericano* airplane?" the chief mechanic inquired. "That thing is
almost forty years old."

"Are you telling me that your section has failed to
see to the maintenance of that craft?" Mark demanded
vehemently. "That's not what *Coronel* Santos or I, or
Presidente Guevara were told. Who's responsible for
this gross negligence? You?"

"*¿Presidente* Guevara?" the chief gasped.

"Aren't you familiar with the chain of command?"
Mark rolled his eyes with frustration. "*El Presidente*
gave the order to *Coronel* Santos, who in turn contacted me not five minutes ago by telephone. The
message was in code, of course, and I just deciphered
it. You don't know who I am exactly, but I'm certain
you have some idea, no?"

"Well, yes," the chief began awkwardly. "There has
been talk about you, *capitán*—"

"Then you know I have top security clearance at
this installation and I'm working directly with *General*—
ah, *Coronel* Santos, who is acting under the direct
orders of *Presidente* Guevara. Do I understand that
you are refusing a direct order from *el Presidente*?"

"No, no, *¡capitán!*" the chief mechanic assured him.
"We'll have the plane ready immediately, *capitán*."

"*Bueno,*" Mark snapped. "I'll mention you favorably
in my report." Coolly, the Penetrator started to walk
away.

"Ah," a timid voice called to him. "With what are we
to arm it, *señor capitán*?"

Mark affected a glower. "Charge the machine guns,

naturally. Napalm bombs, and load the wing racks with the *norteamericano* Terrier air-to-ground missiles."

"Sí, Señor Capitán, immediatamente."

Half an hour later, the flight crew watched with satisfaction as the AT-6-F fighter rolled down the runway and rose into the air. The plane climbed higher and sailed into the sky. A smile on his face, the chief mechanic turned to see Colonel Santos arrive in his jeep, accompanied by three military policemen with rifles at the ready. The chief jogged over to the colonel and saluted.

"I am pleased to report that your orders have been carried out and all has gone well, *general*," he declared.

Santos returned the salute and glared at the mechanic. "What orders? And why are you addressing me as general?"

"The orders you gave *capitán* Chaney—"

Santos exploded. "Chaney! Where is that *gringo hijo de puta*?"

"General?" the chief's smile faded. "We shouldn't have let him take the airplane?"

"Airplane?" Santos trembed with rage. "You *estúpido*! You let Chaney fly out of here in one of our planes?"

"Sí," the mechanic admitted reluctantly. "Isn't *capitán* Chaney acting on your orders and the orders of *Presidente* Guevara, general?"

"I've just had a meeting with Guevara."

"Ah, *sí*," the mechanic sighed out with relief.

"*El Presidente* checked with his sources at Langley," Santos began in an angry voice. "This man Chaney wasn't sent by the CIA. That *hijo de la chingada* is an imposter! We were ordered to place him under arrest and now you tell me he just flew away in one of our planes?"

"Ah—*sí, general*," the chief admitted sheepishly.

"Don't call me general!" Santos snapped. "I'm never going to see a promotion after today! I'll be lucky if I don't face a court-martial. *¡Madre de Dios!* I may be lucky not to face *el peredón*." Santos calmed himself. "Did Chaney tell you where he was taking the plane? Do you have any idea?"

"No, gen—*coronel*," the mechanic corrected nervously. He saw his stripes flying away with the renegade American. "But, maybe I should mention something. It might be important."

"*Anything* will help," Santos growled furiously. "Nothing you can say can make this situation any worse."

"We—we armed the plane with napalm bombs and Terrier missiles," the chief admitted, speaking rapidly in an effort to avoid the colonel's rage by giving the news to him quickly.

Santos's mouth fell open. "*¡Mierda!*" he gasped in a defeated tone.

The Penetrator checked the instrument panel of the AT-6-F with satisfaction. "Old girl's doing fine," he remarked. "Always wanted to fly one of these crates, but I never figured I'd wind up stealing one to do it." Mark's pleasure was starkly contrasted by the vital importance of his mission and the dangerous circumstances involved in his unauthorized flight. He glanced at the compass. The most logical and least hazardous choice of action was to head southeast into Honduras. Flying over El Salvador would have been like riding a hang glider into the eye of a hurricane. Everybody was shooting at everyone else in El Salvador and anything in the skies would be apt to be considered fair game by all sides. Next, the Penetrator recalled the key locations of Soviet-made antiaircraft weapons in Nicaragua.

Most were along the border at El Salvador—yet another reason not to take that route. Others were positioned along the coast and at Diriamba near Lake Nicaragua. Most of the country's fighter planes were at

Sandino near the capital and Bluefields. None of them had been based near the mountain range where the Plague Five complex was hidden. The less of Nicaragua he'd have to fly over, the better. The Guatemalan air force charts gave him a good course. Cutting across Honduras seemed the best way to go—providing they didn't shoot him down.

They didn't.

Although Mark flew low whenever possible to avoid radar detection, twice he received radio messages from Hounduran air traffic controllers. Fortunately, Central American communications are less sophisticated than in the United States, and the air controllers aren't as well trained.

On the first contact, Mark managed to bluff his way out of trouble by giving them answers that seemed to make sense.

"Aircraft in the vicinity of Estili," crackled an English-speaking voice on Mark's radio. "Do you have a transponder?"

"*¿Qué?*" the Penetrator returned in Spanish.

"Please identify yourself, you are about to enter Nicaraguan airspace," the speaker went on patiently. "If you do not have a transponder, please designate your aircraft type and number, point of origin, and destination by voice."

The Penetrator affected a heavy Spanish accent to his English words. "I am Major Luis Platos-Ocampo of the army of La República de México. Please repeat all after 'please designate.' Over."

With consummate control, the ground operator placidly reviewed his instructions, adding at the end, "Are you flying a military aircraft?"

"*¡Ay de mí!*" Mark replied. "No. I am in my private craft. Over."

"What is your airspeed and destination?"

"Please repeat all after 'what is.' I have the trouble with my radio."

The farce went on for five more minutes, while the big radial engine bellowed, bringing Mark closer to Matagalpa. Then he put the hooker in.

"I am flying at two hundred seventy knots."

An awed response came back, "What is it you have, *Señor Mayor*?"

"A Mustang I purchased from my government when they got the jets from the *gringos*."

Let them look for a P-51 Mustang, the Penetrator thought. His gull-wing bird would hardly fit the description. He could fly much faster, too. That should put the search far behind him by the time they realized their error.

The second call came from right on the Nicaraguan border. A dose of the same double-talk seemed to work. Civilian and military air traffic controllers would probably still be trying to figure out exactly what he had said when he attacked the Plague Five base.

By flying low, Mark could avoid electronic detection, but he was still visible to observation teams and ground forces. The Penetrator glanced down at the startled, disoriented Sandinistan troops that suddenly appeared below. Several soldiers aimed their rifles at the plane, hesitated, and held their fire. The cross-shaped shadow of the AT-6-F flashed across the massive barrel of a Soviet antiaircraft gun.

"Nuts," Mark said through clenched teeth. "That's not supposed to be here."

His thumb moved toward the firing mechanism, prepared to swing around and strafe the gun below. Then he noticed the soldiers stationed at the weapon were waving their arms frantically. One man knelt by a field radio, probably calling for instructions.

The Penetrator grinned. The Sandinistans didn't know what to do. After all, a single plane—and an old one at that—had flown across the border in broad daylight. This hardly seemed to be a genuine attack. Even the Sandinistans were reluctant to shoot down an aircraft that had simply made a mistake. Particularly if such an incident could be the spark to set off war with Honduras and possibly her neighbors as well.

Nicaragua didn't want a full-scale war—at least, not until it was ready for one. Likewise, Mark didn't want to make any aggressive move unless he had to. The Penetrator had no desire to trigger a major conflict in Central America, but nothing could stand in the way of his mission.

On the ground below, a Cuban major shrieked at the Nicaraguan troops and demanded to know why they allowed the plane to cross the border. The soldiers were unable to reply. One of them decided to try to rectify the error and raised a fiberglass rocket launcher to his shoulder. The Sandinistan tried to get the departing aircraft in his sights, but the Cuban ordered him to put the weapon down. The plane had already passed far out of range for anything to hit. If the rocket launcher missed, its HE projectile would be apt to fall on the billets below. The Cuban cursed the inefficiency of the Nicaraguans. He almost ordered the antiaircraft gun turned around, then decided that was pointless. If the airplane was friendly, it made no difference. If it proved hostile, chances were it would be shot down elsewhere and certainly would never come back the same way it entered. By that time the plane had become a dark pinprick in the sky, headed toward the mountains and jungles to the east.

Colonel Po marched into the radio room in the headquarters building of his hidden stronghold. Lieutenant Chung had told him an urgent message from Colonel Montoya had that minute arrived and the Sandinistan officer demanded to speak to Po personally. The Chinese colonel waved the radio operator out of the room and sat down by the machine. Although furious with Montoya's breach of security by such direct radio contact, he kept his temper in check as he adjusted the headset and spoke into the microphone.

"High Commander. Over," he announced in a flat, hard voice.

"This is Night Bird," Montoya's voice replied through the static. "I read you, High Commander. Over."

"Did you acquire identification of personnel discussed in previous transmission? Over." Po referred to the bodies of Lieutenant Escutia and Sergeant Mudeja, which had been examined after the assault on the Plague Five installation three nights before.

"Affirmative," Montoya stated. "Personnel identified as former members of Somoza *guardia nacional*. Believed to be working with other exiles somewhere to the north. Probably Honduras. Strong possibility assault was action of guerrillas belonging to the National Army of Liberation, commanded by Juan Carlos. Over."

Po clucked his tongue in disgust. Such information hardly merited the risk in radio contact. "Have you anything else to report, Night Bird? Over."

"Affirmative, High Commander. Fifteen minutes ago, I learned a lone plane crossed the Honduras border into Nicaragua. Does not appear to be contemporary military aircraft. It seems to be flying beneath radar scans, so a definite confirmation of its current position is not possible at this time. Reports suggest the craft, possibly a *norteamericano* AT-6-F fighter plane, is heading toward the jungle. May be approaching your location. Over."

"Approaching our location," Po whispered. He didn't speak into the microphone. *"The Penetrator!"*

The muffled roar of an explosion outside the building suddenly confirmed the colonel's fears.

Po abandoned the radio and bolted into the corridor to discover armed troops, lab technicians, and Third World representatives darting frantically through the hallway.

Colonel Po headed to the front entrance and stared out at the long greenhouse wings of the insect-breeding complex. Flames completely consumed an entire section. The giant vulture shape of an airplane shadow swept across the remaining portion of the installation. He heard the buzz of the plane's engine above the crackle of flames and the shouts of frightened men.

The fighter slewed through the sky and lined up for a second pass, giving Po a good look at the dark metallic belly of the AT-6-F. It suddenly dived low over the complex, swooped up sharply, and rose, dropping two oval-shaped objects. Po watched the plane climb and swing away from the target area an instant before the bombs exploded.

A mushroom of fire burst from the center of another insect-breeding wing. Napalm covered the "greenhouse" and filled its interior with molten destruction.

Machine guns snarled. Two teams of Sandinistans had set up a pair of M-60s, the barrels propped against the porch railings to elevate the aim of their weapons. Belts of ammunition coiled through the machine guns and hot cartridge casings hopped from the breech of each gun. Brilliant red tracer rounds popped across the sky. The machine gunners cursed and shifted the M-60s, desperately trying to get a steady bead on the elusive fighter plane.

The Penetrator gazed through the Plexiglas window of the AT-6-F and saw the twin flames of orange from the enemy machine guns at the barracks. The M-60 wasn't designed to fire at aircraft, but it still had an impressive range and could eat prodigious amounts of ammunition. The ominous *clang, clang* of projectiles biting into the metal skin of the plane warned Mark that the enemy could hit him and might well be able to bring him down.

With grim determination, the Penetrator eased the stick forward and lowered the nose of the AT-6-F. The bellowing roar of the diving plane filled his ears and the barracks drew closer. The machine guns kept spitting rounds at him, accompanied by the M-16s of other soldiers who joined their comrades in the defense. Mark placed a thumb to a red button and pressed.

Two Terrier missiles screamed when they shot from under the wings of the plane. A pair of long, white streaks trailed behind the projectiles like the tails of lethal comets. All eyes of the men at the Plague Five installation watched in horror—none more so than the terrified troops at the barracks. The missiles smashed into the billets. An earth-shaking, soul-shattering explosion burst throughout the complex. The barracks errupted into flying debris of charred wood, mangled metal, and grotesque human limbs. All that remained of the building consisted of twisted, smoldering, lifeless wreckage.

"Wang pu tan!" Colonel Po cried in outrage. He turned to face Lieutenant Chung. "I want that plane shot out of the sky immediately."

Comrade colonel," Chung began in a dazed tone. "All the Sandinistan soldiers were in the barracks. They're all dead. All we have are scientists, technicians, some security personnel, and our comrades from other nations—"

"They can still pull the trigger of a gun," Po snapped. "We are all soldiers for the cause of world Communism—and anyone who refuses to fight will be executed on the spot!"

"No need for such a drastic measure," Dr. Kassem, the Arab entomologist, assured him in a pleasant voice.

"Professor Kowdow and I have taken care of the problem for you."

The colonel glared at Kassem, who stood calmly with his hands in the pockets of a white smock, a confident smile on his swarthy face. "What do you mean?" Po demanded.

"Comrade," the Arab sighed with disappointment. "Plague Five is the greatest weapon of all time. We're going to conquer the entire Western Hemisphere with it. Do you think one antique airplane and a few bombs are any match for such technology?"

"Look out there!" Po screamed, thrusting a finger at the flaming breeding complex. "Your precious insects are burning up like suicidal Buddhist monks!"

"Insects are the most abundant creatures on the planet," Kassem shrugged. "Their supply is limitless and our opponent has only put a dent in their number. You'll see."

As though to verify the entomologist's claims, a high-pitched whine suddenly wailed from loudspeakers within the installation. Instantly, a dense cloud whirled into the sky. Millions of locusts rose in a tornado-shaped pattern, fanning out as they approached the AT-6-F above.

"I believe," Kassem mused with a cruel grin, "flying conditions have suddenly become most unfavorable."

The Penetrator couldn't have disagreed with the Arab's prediction. Mark had not heard the siren, but he immediately recognized the danger the minute the locusts appeared. The insects materialized with incredible speed.

One moment the sky shone crystal clear and blue, the next it had been opaqued with thousands of small, winged creatures. Locusts smashed into the windshield and splattered their innards across the Plexiglas. Hopelessly, Mark turned on the wipers, but it only served to increase the smear of insect guts that seemed to paint the window and blind his view.

Mark heard the engine sputter and felt the plane tremble like a great wounded beast. Hundreds of locusts had entered and clogged the air intakes. The instruments started telling him impossible things and he realized the Pitot tube had also been jammed with crushed bugs. Might as well try to fly through a giant pool of Jell-O, Mark thought. He rapidly lost control of the AT-6-F. Every window of the craft had been covered by the splattered corpses of thousands of locusts, and, with the static air instruments out, including the altimeter and artificial horizon, he didn't know if he was right side up or not. Now, the enemy could blast him out of the sky while he remained helpless to launch any kind of counterattack.

Colonel Po smiled when he saw the AT-6-F wobble away from the installation. The plane swung awkwardly over the jungle beyond, a blinded, wounded eagle in search of a place to die. He turned to Dr. Kassem and bowed.

"My compliments to you and Professor Kowdow," he said in a respectful voice. "Now, Plague Five can continue as planned." The colonel glanced up at the retreating shape of the crippled plane. A beatific smile spread over his saturnine features.

"A pity the Penetrator was not born Chinese. He was, I admit, a most worthy adversary."

17

KILL A MONSTER

Any attempt to blindly land an airplane would be enormously dangerous. To try to do so in an environment of jungle trees and mountains was downright suicidal. Mark eased back the throttle. The Penetrator had to see where he was before he could decide what to do next.

He reached for the emergency release handle, removed the arming-wire safety, and jerked. Explosive pops sounded and the greenhouse flew up and rearward. At least he could see to the sides. He rose and hazarded a forward glance around the smeared windshield.

The Penetrator stared into the tombstone-gray surface of a mountain.

Instantly, Mark veered to the left. The rock walls seemed to move with his craft, determined to block his escape and smash him to bits. Then the edge of the mountain crept into view. Mark dropped the left wing in what he hoped would be a sixty-degree bank—any more and he faced the danger of slipping into a staggering, sideways stall. The tip of the right wing nearly brushed the stony obstacle when the sheer granite surface flashed past. Still too fast, Mark thought, then eased back on the throttle more.

Mark wiped the back of one hand across his brow, mopping a thick film of cold sweat. The near collision with the mountain had been too close—and he still had plenty of problems to cope with. The air intakes and Pitot tube were still clogged with dead locusts. He had lost his instruments and the big radial power-house could die at any second. At least he'd flown beyond the swarm of kamikaze insects—otherwise they'd be pouring into the open cockpit.

The old AT-6-F rattled and shook violently. Mark eased the seat to a midway position, so that his head and shoulders cleared the sides of the fuselage. He gazed down at the clusters of treetops below, desperately searching for a large, flat area suitable for an emergency landing. His toes barely actuated the rudder peddles and he controlled the stick with fingertips. Experimentally, he wobbled the wings, then dropped the left to get a better look at the ground below.

To his amazement, he passed a forest of rubber trees and giant ferns and stared down at the most beautiful sight he'd encountered in Nicaragua. A small dirt runway, located near a shabby farmhouse and an old barn, lay stretched out before him like a mirage in the desert. The place appeared to be abandoned, probably the former property of a local bush pilot who'd fled the country after the Sandinistans took over and made free enterprise unprofitable and unhealthy.

Mark nearly wept with relief. He circled around the strip, surprised and pleased to discover it was nearly 3,600 feet long, before he lowered the nose to descend. He dropped the flaps and landing gear and drew the throttle back, rejoicing. The little airfield not only offered a safe landing but a place to repair his craft and take off afterward—provided he could remain alive to do so.

"One thing at a time," the Penetrator told himself while he lined up with the runway, eased back the stick, and checked the throttle again. He could still lose it, land ten feet below the strip or ground loop and explode the remaining rockets. Just a piece of cake!

*   *   *

Doctor Raymond Barr pulled his face away from the twin eyepieces of the microscope and shook his head with despair. Dr. Gomara looked at the American and frowned. The Mexican entomologist had grown to like Barr, though he remained a dedicated Marxist, devoted to the goals of the Third World and international Communism. Since the missile attack on the barracks had killed the troops stationed at the complex, Colonel Po had ordered Gomara and the other scientists to guard the rebellious Dr. Barr until Montoya could send reinforcements.

Gomara warned himself not to become too fond of the *gringo*. His duty to the cause was more important than personal friendship, and Raymond Barr's life would end as soon as his usefulness to the project expired. Gomara hooked his thumbs in the web belt buckled around his wide girth. The .45 Obregon pistol on his hip felt awkward, heavy, and totally alien.

"I'm simply at a loss as to how we can go about synthetic reproduction of this arachnid pheromone," Barr announced in a weary voice. He placed his fingertips to his temples and massaged them while he gazed up at Gomara. "I could sure use a drink, *amigo*."

The Mexican glanced about the laboratory. He and Barr were alone in the room. Professor Kowdow, Dr. Kassem, and the others were still inspecting the damage to the breeding wings. He didn't see any suitable sharp or heavy instruments available that Barr might try to use as a weapon. Silly notion, he thought. Barr didn't have the stomach or the backbone to kill anyone at close quarters. Besides, Gomara had a gun.

"I've got some rum in my desk," Gomara confessed. "I'll let you have one drink to steady your nerves, *¿comprehende?* Just one."

"Sure, Rafael," Barr nodded eagerly. "That's all I need."

Gomara bobbed his head in reply. One is never enough for an alcoholic, but he'd humor the poor Anglo fool. The Mexican waddled to his desk. His back turned to Barr, Gomara didn't see the American quickly slip on a pair of thick rubber gloves.

Barr quietly slid off his stool and stealthfully walked to a small aluminum table that contained numerous test tubes, beakers, and the wire cage with the giant Bahamian centipede inside. Keeping a watchful eye on the unsuspecting Gomara, Barr placed a trembling hand on the door of the cage and thumbed back its latch.

Raymond Barr knew he had to act fast—before the others returned, before Gomara could turn around, and before his own nerve broke. He reached into the cage and seized the eighteen-inch-long centipede in both gloved hands.

"Ah!" Gomara declared, raising a half-full bottle of dark liquid. "Here we go—"

He turned in mid-sentence to see Raymond Barr charge. The American held the hideous Bahamian giant like a spear, his arms outstretched, prepared for a lunge. Gomara dropped the rum and attempted a clumsy draw, his fingers fumbling with the button-flap holster on his sidearm. He realized his error too late.

Barr closed in swiftly and shoved the bulbous head of the centipede into the side of the Mexican's neck.

Gomara screamed when sharp fangs sank into his flesh and pierced the carotid artery. Barr released the centipede. Its numerous legs clung to Gomara's shoulder, its fangs still embedded in his neck, pumping venom. Gomara's hands clawed at the slimy creature. He staggered backward, tripped over a stool, and crashed to the floor. Barr felt his stomach heave while he watched Gomara's body thrash in wild convulsions before death ended his agony.

Barr seized a Bunsen burner, turned up its flame,

and knelt beside Gomara's corpse to thrust the blue gas blaze into the centipede's head. The creature twisted and curled under the concentrated bolt of fire. Barr burned the Bahamian giant until he was certain no life remained in the monstrous centipede.

"I'll be damned," he gasped, his heart racing and his hands unsteady from tension. "It worked."

Barr realized he had only accomplished the first part of his plan. With quivering fingers, he unbuttoned the holster on Gormara's hip and extracted the big Obregon pistol. Barr glanced at the giant terrariums that contained a lethal assortment of the most terrifying products of the insect world. Aware that time was running out fast and the others would soon return, he rose and walked to the cabinet of pheromone bottles.

Professor Kowdow, Dr. Kassem, four security officers, and the three representatives of various Third World nations who had remained at the installation strolled back to the headquarters building. The entomologists had assured the trio of covert diplomats that the damage to the breeding wings of the complex wouldn't put an end to Operation Plague Five.

"The Western Hemisphere has a plentiful supply of destructive insects," Kassem explained. "Now that we've mastered the necessary pheromonal controls, we can use the creatures native to this part of the world to carry out the mission."

"I suppose that's true enough," Robert M'Nobi, the representative from Mozambique, sighed with regret. "Still, it's a bloody pity that we went to so much trouble to transport some of my country's least desirable crawling beasties for the purpose of this project."

"The *siafu, tsetse* flies, and other African species will still be used, comrade," Kowdow stated, reaching for the door. "They reproduce rapidly, and in our controlled environment we can breed millions within a few months. The same, of course, applies to the Hymenoptera X strain of superwasps we developed." The Korean pulled open the door, his face still turned to the other men as he spoke.

Kowdow didn't hear the angry whirr of wings or see the black-and-yellow creatures that shot through the doorway like machine-gun bullets. He did feel two wasps land lightly on his cheek and right ear. Needles of pain pierced his flesh. The Korean screamed, stunned by the toxic stingers that struck twice more before the wasps abandoned Kowdow to join their fellow hornets in another attack.

"Wasp X," Kowdow muttered with amazing calmness in his native language, while he stumbled inside the building. "Stingers—fatal—need an injection—epinephrine hydrochloride—immediately . . ." Then he swooned and toppled against the doorway.

Kowdow sprawled across the threshold, his corpse jamming open the door. His face and neck had already swollen horribly from the poison, but the Korean wouldn't suffocate. His heart had already stopped beating.

The eight men who'd accompanied Kowdow didn't notice his demise. They were too busy trying to avoid a similar fate. Panic-stricken, they ran—even Dr. Kassem, who fully realized the futility of trying to race against insects capable of flying forty-five miles per hour.

The wasps swooped down on the men before they could reach any sort of shelter. Stingers sunk into necks, hands, and faces. Unlike bees, the wasps had smooth stingers that allowed them to strike repeatedly—and the hymenoptera X had been specially bred and nourished to be aggressive, sturdy, and deadly.

"*Haqui*—fuck you—*Qaddafi!*" Yassine Fawhi, the Libyan representative screamed after he'd been stung in the side of the neck by three hornets. His uttered curse for the man who'd sent him to Nicaragua proved to be Fawhi's last words.

Dr. Kassem stopped running and sat down on the ground. His skull pulsated painfully and lumps of poisoned flesh ballooned at the back of his head. The Arab removed a pack of cigarettes and shook one out. No point in running. He'd be dead in three or four minutes anyway. Kassem watched the others flee into the jungle, joined by the technicians who had been inspecting the damaged breeding wings. A thick black cloud of wasps pursued them. Kassem stuck the cigarette in his mouth and wondered what death would be like. He found out before he could use his lighter.

Inside the headquarters building, Raymond Barr cautiously stepped from the laboratory. He wore a special reinforced beekeeper's suit and mask and held the Obregon .45 in a thickly gloved fist. After donning the protective apparel, Barr had pheromonally programmed the hornets to attack and released the killer wasps. The screams of the insects' victims gradually subsided. Surprised that he felt more determination than fear, Barr moved into the corridor to finish off anyone who managed to survive the wasp attack.

Dr. Raymond Barr felt the bullet smash into his back at the same instant he heard the sharp report of a pistol behind him. Despite the burning pain and shock, Barr tried to pivot and fire back at his assailant. Two more 95-grain, jacketed hollow-point slugs struck the doctor, propelling him across the corridor. Barr's chest and wire-mesh covered face slapped into a wall while a fourth .380 caliber round burrowed under his left shoulder blade and into his heart.

"Louise?" Barr whispered. He wondered if his wife waited for him in the next life. Then Dr. Raymond Barr's corpse slid down the face of the wall and slumped to the floor.

Colonel Po approached the pile of thick canvas and

lifeless flesh, the Astra Constable still in his fist. Angrily, he pumped the last two bullets into the back of Barr's helmeted head. Po heard rushing footsteps on the stairwell at the end of the corridor. Lieutenant Chung bounded down the last three steps. A white plastic breathing mask covered the lieutenant's nose and mouth and he held a large cylinder of insecticide with a long nozzle in his hands.

"What is wrong, comrade colonel?" Chung inquired, his voice muffled by the mask.

He has to ask? Po thought with annoyance, then replied. "Many things." He shoved the empty Astra into its holster. He had no need to reload it. All their shootable enemies were now dead. "Our suspicions were correct, lieutenant. Barr released the wasps. That lunatic! I should have killed him weeks ago."

"It is fortunate we were in your office with the door closed when the hornets filled the building," Chung stated, trying to minimize the disaster.

Po heard an automatic weapon snarl somewhere outside the building. "Those fools must be shooting at the wasps," he growled and shook his head.

"I found a few wasps upstairs," Chung reported. He raised a can of insecticide. "They are all dead now."

"Did anyone else survive the attack?" Po asked, his eyes ablaze with fury.

"No, comrade colonel," the lieutenant admitted.

Po's body trembled with rage. First the Penetrator destroys half the complex and most of his men, and then Dr. Barr wipes out what remained. It would take months to get enough trained personnel to replace the slain members of the operation. Peking would be furious when it learned of this setback.

"Check inside the laboratory," the colonel instructed. "I'll radio Montoya and find out when he can get some more troops to us."

"*Hau, hau,* comrade colonel," Chung replied quickly. He jogged into the lab, holding the spray can like a machine gun.

The colonel spat on Raymond Barr's corpse. Ruined! No, he chided himself. It would take time to rebuild, but Operation Plague Five could still succeed.

"Congratulations, Colonel Po," a hard, cold voice announced in English.

Po looked up with a start and saw the tall, lean figure of the Penetrator approach from the entrance of the HQ building. Mark held an empty M-16 in his left hand and the .45 MatchMaster in his right. He let the rifle fall to the floor to grip the pistol in both hands.

"You look just like your photographs," Mark said in a vehement, soft voice. "And Vietnam was ten years ago. You do remember Nam, don't you?"

"So you survived the plane crash, Mr. Penetrator," Po commented, raising his hands in surrender.

"Makes us even," Mark replied as he stepped closer. "You left Hanoi a few hours before I could carry out my mission to assassinate you, Po. I was afraid I'd never get a chance to make up for that mistake."

"Fate is inscrutable," the colonel remarked, taking a step backward. "One is not without hope until the last shot has been fired."

"Well, listen up, colonel," the Penetrator hissed. He raised the MatchMaster and aimed it at Po's face. "You're about to hear the last shot—*for you.*"

Colonel Po's coy smile warned Mark that something had gone wrong. He saw an object move out of the corner of his eye and turned to see Lieutenant Chung at the theshold of the laboratory. The young Chinese officer held a 7.65 Tokarev automatic, pointed at the Penetrator's head.

Chung's finger began to squeeze the trigger . . .

18

TWILIGHT OF THE DAMNED

Instantly the Penetrator reacted.

There wasn't time to think, consider alternatives, or speculate. Years of training and experience took command of his nerves and muscles to respond to the unexpected threat faster than conscious thought would allow.

Mark Hardin pivoted. He bent his knees to lower his body and tilted to one side while he swung the MatchMaster toward the Chinese lieutenant and squeezed the trigger. His movements were fast and smoothly coordinated, accomplishing action simultaneously. The Tokarev in Chung's grasp barked and a bullet hissed past the Penetrator's ear a fragment of a second before the .45 boomed in response.

A big 185-grain hollow-point projectile hit Lieutenant Chung in the face. His right eyeball burst like a blood-filled grape. The orbital bone cracked as the bullet slammed through the eye socket to enter Chung's brain. The lieutenant died on his feet and fell to the floor without uttering another sound.

"Haiiii-yii!" Colonel Po screamed. He launched himself forward and slashed the knifehand edge of his palm into the Penetrator's wrist, striking the ulna nerve. The MatchMaster hopped from Mark's fingers and dropped onto the carpeted floor.

The Penetrator ducked under Po's other hand, which swung a deadly chop at his temple. Striking like twin bolts of lightning, Mark swept a *uraken* backfist to the colonel's face and *nakadaka ippon ken* punch to Po's solar plexus.

The Chinese officer had been well trained in *wu shu* martial arts. Although dazed, he continued his attack and whipped a knee for Mark's groin while his fingers arched into vicious claws that slashed toward his opponent's face. The knee kick hit the Penetrator on the hip and he managed to dodge the twin "tiger claw" stroke, but the force of Po's charge sent him off balance. Mark tripped over the corpse of Lieutenant Chung. He fell backward, into the lab, with Colonel Po right on top of him.

Mark seized Po's wrists and twisted the gouging fingers away from his eyes. His back struck the tile floor hard; yet he managed to lift a foot into the colonel's abdomen. The Penetrator pulled his adversary's arms and straightened his knee to send Po hurtling overhead in a *tomoe-nage* circle throw.

Po struck the floor with spine-jarring force while a metal object skidded across the carpet until it connected with a wall. The MatchMaster .45 had been forcibly shoved across the room during the scuffle.

The Penetrator leaped upright and charged his opponent, determined to kill Po with his bare hands. The colonel rolled into a table and rose with a metal stool in his grasp. Mark saw the sturdy piece of furniture rocketing toward his face and turned in time to take the blow on his shoulder and triceps.

The impact knocked the Penetrator backward. He stumbled into a cabinetful of gallon bottles of yellowish pheromone liquids. Po snarled and raised the stool once more. Mark's hand flashed into the cabinet, grabbed a bottle, and instantly hurled it at his assailant.

The container struck the edge of the stool seat and split open. Pheromones splattered Po's face and the front of his uniform tunic. Temporarily blinded, he threw the stool at Mark. It smacked into the side of the cabinet and bounced to the floor.

Po didn't see the *mae geri keage* snap kick Mark launched to his midsection. The colonel's colon seemed to explode and he doubled up and raised his arms to fend off the next blow while trying to blink the bio-chemicals from his eyes. Po moved a forearm to block the Penetrator's *shuto* chop, aimed at his throat. Then he hooked his other arm in a high arch and stamped the heel of his palm against the side of Mark's head.

The blow filled the Penetrator's skull with bursting hot lights. He staggered toward the row of giant terrariums, slapped a palm against the glass to check his involuntary motion, and braced himself as Po lunged forward, hands poised like eagle's talons.

Mark's leg flashed in a high *mae geri kekomi* side kick. The bottom of his paratrooper boot slammed into Colonel Po's face. The tremendous blow shattered three teeth and broke Po's nose, the force propelling the colonel across the laboratory. He fell into a wall and slumped to the floor, blood gushing from his mouth and nostrils.

The Penetrator caught his breath and prepared to move in for the kill when he saw a twisted smile suddenly appear on Po's scarlet-stained, torn lips. The colonel's hand closed around the grips of the displaced MatchMaster. He swung the pistol up from the floor, hastily aimed it at Mark, and fired. A big .45 slug struck the terrarium near the Penetrator's head. Glass burst and a spiderweb pattern appeared. Mark threw himself to the floor and two more shots missed their target, shattering the thick pane of the terrarium.

Glass shards showered the Penetrator's prone form. Po hadn't been trained to fire a .45 auto, hence his poor marksmanship with the big handgun. Still, they were close enough to compensate for the colonel's lack of skill. The Penetrator cursed under his breath and tried to reach the only weapon left on his person, the Bowie-Axe. He had no illusions about the odds he faced; yet perhaps he could still take Colonel Po with him to the grave.

Suddenly Po screamed.

Mark glanced up to see Po staring at the hole in the glass wall of the terrarium. A column of large, brown ants were filing out of the impromptu exit. The Penetrator felt bolts of icy fear streak through his body as he watched the seemingly endless flow of African driver ants march from the container. Thousands of the deadly creatures swarmed across the floor of the laboratory. *We're both finished,* he thought, aware that there was nothing he could do against the inhuman army of murderous mandibles.

Yet, to his astonishment, the ants completely ignored him. The *siafu* formed a thick, steady line that headed directly for Colonel Po. Panic-stricken, the Chinese officer pointed the MatchMaster at the ants and hopelessly fired down at them until the slide locked back when the last cartridge had been spent. He might as well have tried to spit on the driver ants.

The insects crawled up his pant legs. Po slapped at the *siafu,* which only served to help the ants climb up his arms and chest. Within seconds, the colonel was covered from head to toe by the tiny yet invincible army. Mark watched, fascinated. Po appeared to be a humanoid being with bristles of creeping brown scales for flesh.

The colonel screamed again. Driver ants entered his open mouth. Then they began to bite in unison.

Po's arms flailed desperately. He stumbled and fell to his knees. A strangled gasp emitted from his clogged throat and he clawed at his face, which had already been reduced to shreds, blood pouring from empty eyesockets. Colonel Po Hahn Chau crashed to the floor and convulsed in agony while the driver ants continued their feast.

The Penetrator pulled himself to his feet and staggered from the laboratory, his knees weak, head spinning, and his stomach threatening to erupt through his dry throat. At the doorway, he glanced down to the floor and saw a column of driver ants were now headed toward the damaged bottle of pheromones Mark had hurled at Po during the battle. He noticed a label on the container—SUBFAMILY MYRMICINAE. The fire ant.

Mark understood why the *siafu* had ignored him and attacked Po. The insects were unable to resist the pheromonal command of the biochemicals splashed on the colonel's face and uniform. Driver ants are totally blind and respond entirely to pheromonal impulses. Po had been identified as a colony of fire ants. The Penetrator recalled that only two creatures in the animal kingdom wage war on their own kind—men and ants.

Mark flew the battered old AT-6-F over the jungles of Nicaragua. After a few minor repairs and a hasty washing of the windshield air intakes and digging out the Pitot, the craft proved serviceable. He located an underground tank of stored avgas and refueled, using a large funnel and a chamois to strain out accumulated moisture. Departing the country would be safer than flying into it had been, although he'd have to come up with a good story for the Honduras authorities. He would leave for the States from there. He had decided it wouldn't be terribly healthy to return to Guatemala for a while.

Mark passed over the remains of the Plague Five complex. Flames still crackled across the buildings. He'd located the installation's supply of gasoline and diesel fuel and used it to set fire to the place before he left. The Penetrator wearily patted the thick pile of file folders on the floor in front of him. He had found the complete records of Plague Five in Colonel Po's office. He now had everything he would need to locate and destroy the few small bases that remained in the United States, Mexico, and Canada.

Although there was still some work to be done, the mission itself had been a success and the immediate threat to the Western Hemisphere no longer existed. In another month or two, the Penetrator would have finished the necessary mopping up of Po's scattered forces. Then the only nightmares connected with the operation would be the ones Mark knew would visit him occasionally in his sleep for the rest of his life.

He forced his mind from the grim task that lay ahead and the horrible memories of all he'd seen and experienced in the last few weeks. Mark's thoughts turned to Angie and the kids, the best mental and emotional balm in the world. Yeah, he thought. When it was all over, he knew where to go for a terrific hot tub, a superb pool, and lots of badly needed tender loving care.

DEATH MERCHANT

by Joseph Rosenberger

**More bestselling action/adventure
from Pinnacle, America's #1 series publisher—
Over 14 million copies in print!**

☐ 41-345-9 Death Merchant #1	$1.95	☐ 41-383-1 The Fourth Reich #39	$1.95
☐ 41-346-7 Operation Overkill #2	$1.95	☐ 41-019-0 Shamrock Smash #41	$1.75
☐ 41-347-5 Psychotron Plot #3	$1.95	☐ 41-020-4 High Command Murder #42	$1.95
☐ 41-348-3 Chinese Conspiracy #4	$1.95	☐ 41-021-2 Devil's Trashcan #43	$1.95
☐ 41-349-1 Satan Strike #5	$1.95	☐ 41-326-2 The Rim of Fire	
☐ 41-350-5 Albanian Connection #6	$1.95	Conspiracy #45	$1.95
☐ 41-351-3 Castro File #7	$1.95	☐ 41-327-0 Blood Bath #46	$1.95
☐ 41-352-1 Billionaire Mission #8	$1.95	☐ 41-328-9 Operation Skyhook #47	$1.95
☐ 41-353-X Laser War #9	$1.95	☐ 41-644-X The Psionics War #48	$1.95
☐ 41-354-8 Mainline Plot #10	$1.95	☐ 41-645-8 Night of the Peacock #49	$1.95
☐ 41-378-5 Operation Mind-Murder #34	$1.95	☐ 41-657-1 The Hellbomb Theft #50	$2.25
☐ 41-380-7 Cosmic Reality Kill #36	$1.95	☐ 41-658-X The Inca File #51	$2.25
☐ 41-382-3 The Burning		☐ 41-659-8 Flight of The Phoenix #52	$2.25
Blue Death #38	$1.95	☐ 41-660-1 The Judas Scrolls #53	$2.25

Buy them at your local bookstore or use this handy coupon
Clip and mail this page with your order

 PINNACLE BOOKS, INC.—Reader Service Dept.
1430 Broadway, New York, NY 10018

Please send me the book(s) I have checked above. I am enclosing $_____ (please
add 75¢ to cover postage and handling). Send check or money order only—no cash or
C.O.D.'s.

Mr./Mrs./Miss _____

Address _____

City _____ State/Zip _____

Please allow six weeks for delivery. Prices subject to change without notice.

CELEBRATING 10 YEARS IN PRINT
AND OVER 22 MILLION COPIES SOLD!

☐ 41-756-X Created, The Destroyer #1	$2.25
☐ 41-757-8 Death Check #2	$2.25
☐ 41-811-6 Chinese Puzzle #3	$2.25
☐ 41-758-6 Mafia Fix #4	$2.25
☐ 41-220-7 Dr. Quake #5	$1.95
☐ 41-221-5 Death Therapy #6	$1.95
☐ 41-222-3 Union Bust #7	$1.95
☐ 41-814-0 Summit Chase #8	$2.25
☐ 41-224-X Murder's Shield #9	$1.95
☐ 41-225-8 Terror Squad #10	$1.95
☐ 41-856-6 Kill Or Cure #11	$2.25
☐ 41-227-4 Slave Safari #12	$1.95
☐ 41-228-2 Acid Rock #13	$1.95
☐ 41-229-0 Judgment Day #14	$1.95
☐ 41-768-3 Murder Ward #15	$2.25
☐ 41-231-2 Oil Slick #16	$1.95
☐ 41-232-0 Last War Dance #17	$1.95
☐ 40-894-3 Funny Money #18	$1.75
☐ 40-895-1 Holy Terror #19	$1.75
☐ 41-235-5 Assassins Play-Off #20	$1.95
☐ 41-236-3 Deadly Seeds #21	$1.95
☐ 40-898-6 Brain Drain #22	$1.75
☐ 41-884-1 Child's Play #23	$2.25
☐ 41-239-8 King's Curse #24	$1.95
☐ 40-901-X Sweet Dreams #25	$1.75

☐ 40-902-8 In Enemy Hands #26	$1.75
☐ 41-242-8 Last Temple #27	$1.95
☐ 41-243-6 Ship of Death #28	$1.95
☐ 40-905-2 Final Death #29	$1.75
☐ 40-110-8 Mugger Blood #30	$1.50
☐ 40-907-9 Head Men #31	$1.75
☐ 40-908-7 Killer Chromosomes #32	$1.75
☐ 40-909-5 Voodoo Die #33	$1.75
☐ 41-249-5 Chained Reaction #34	$1.95
☐ 41-250-9 Last Call #35	$1.95
☐ 41-251-7 Power Play #36	$1.95
☐ 41-252-5 Bottom Line #37	$1.95
☐ 41-253-3 Bay City Blast #38	$1.95
☐ 41-254-1 Missing Link #39	$1.95
☐ 41-255-X Dangerous Games #40	$1.95
☐ 41-766-7 Firing Line #41	$2.25
☐ 41-767-5 Timber Line #42	$2.25
☐ 41-909-0 Midnight Man #43	$2.25
☐ 40-718-1 Balance of Power #44	$1.95
☐ 40-719-X Spoils of War #45	$1.95
☐ 40-720-3 Next of Kin #46	$1.95
☐ 41-557-5 Dying Space #47	$2.25
☐ 41-558-3 Profit Motive #48	$2.75
☐ 41-559-1 Skin Deep #49	$2.25

Buy them at your local bookstore or use this handy coupon
Clip and mail this page with your order

⊙ **PINNACLE BOOKS, INC. — Reader Service Dept.**
1430 Broadway, New York, NY 10018
Please send me the book(s) I have checked above. I am enclosing $_____ (please add
75¢ to cover postage and handling). Send check or money order only — no cash or C.O.D.'s.

Mr./Mrs./Miss _____

Address _____

City _____ State/Zip _____

Please allow six weeks for delivery. Prices subject to change without notice.